Books by Todd Strasser

Home Alone (novelization)

Home Alone 2 (novelization)

The Diving Bell

The Mall from Outer Space

Beyond the Reef

The Complete Computer Popularity Program

FREE WILLY

A novelization by Todd Strasser
Based on the
Screenplay by Keith A. Walker and Corey Blechman
Story by Keith A. Walker

SCHOLASTIC INC.
New York Toronto London Auckland Sydney

WARNER BROS. PRESENTS

IN ASSOCIATION WITH LE STUDIO CANAL+, REGENCY ENTERPRISES AND ALCOR FILMS A DONNER / SHULER-DONNER PRODUCTION A FILM BY SIMON WINCER

'FREE WILLY' JASON JAMES RICHTER LORI PETTY JAYNE ATKINSON AUGUST SCHELLENBERG AND MICHAEL MADSEN EDITED BY O. NICHOLAS BROWN

PRODUCTION DESIGNED BY CHARLES ROSEN DIRECTOR OF PHOTOGRAPHY ROBBIE GREENBERG, A.S.C. MUSIC BY BASIL POLEDOURIS CO-PRODUCERS PENELOPE FOSTER,

RICHARD SOLOMON AND JIM VAN WYCK EXECUTIVE PRODUCERS RICHARD DONNER AND ARNON MILCHAN STORY BY KEITH A. WALKER

SCREENPLAY BY KEITH A. WALKER AND COREY BLECHMAN PRODUCED BY JENNIE LEW TUGEND AND LAUREN SHULER-DONNER

DOLBY STEREO
IN SELECTED THEATRES   DIRECTED BY SIMON WINCER   WARNER BROS.
A TIME WARNER ENTERTAINMENT COMPANY
© 1993 Warner Bros. All Rights Reserved   WB

ISBN 0-590-46756-5

12 11 10 9 8 7 6 5 4 3   3 4 5 6 7 8/9

Printed in the U.S.A.   40

First Scholastic printing, July 1993

*To David, Ellen, and Marni Weil,
who understand the need for freedom.*

FREE WILLY

1

The blue waters of the ocean were calm at dawn; its surface was like a liquid mirror. To the west, the cloudless sky was a deep, dark blue. But to the east, the sky had turned a shade lighter as the red morning sun began to rise over a thin strip of rough forestland in the distance. There, sheltered by a rocky bay, three boats waited to trap a killer whale.

Not far from the bay, a long, black dorsal fin knifed across the ocean surface. It was followed by another and then another, gliding in graceful arcs up and out and then back into the water. Gradually, the fins rose higher, revealing the broad, slick backs of six whales blowing great bursts of misty spray though blowholes as they broke the surface.

In the rocky bay, the biggest of the three boats, a ragged old brown fishing trawler, chugged slowly in a semicircle, leaving a long rusted metal net in its wake. Once the metal net sank into the water, no living creature larger than a man's fist could swim through it.

A smaller, faster chase boat drifted quietly outside the bay. On the deck, its captain held a pair of binoculars to his weathered face. He had just spotted the tall, black dorsal fins of the whales slicing through the smooth waters toward him. He had been waiting two weeks for this moment. If he succeeded in catching a whale, he would soon earn enough money to buy a new boat. He was determined not to fail.

Swimming playfully through the water, the pod of six killer whales was unaware of the danger that lay ahead. The whales knew each other well. They had been together their entire lives. They had hunted and played together, rubbed each other's bellies with their long, rounded flippers, nursed their baby calves, and come to the aid of each other when they were sick or injured. They were as much a family as that of any two-legged creature who walked on land.

One of the whales was larger than a calf, but not yet fully grown. Like the others, he was jet-black with a gleaming white underbelly and a small white patch behind each eye. But this young whale had special markings that none of the others possessed — three small dark spots under his broad white jaw. And so he was known as Three Spots.

As the whales glided through the cold, clear

waters toward the rocky bay, Three Spots swam ahead, playfully racing in and out of thick fifty-foot-long ribbons of brownish-green kelp.

On the deck of the chase boat, the captain could now see the whales quite clearly as they swam into the bay, unaware that they were surrounded on three sides by the curtain of steel netting.

"Now!" the captain shouted. The chase boat's engines fired up with a roar.

In the water nearby, the pod of swimming whales came to an abrupt halt. Instantly alert, they raced to the surface and poked their black heads out of the water, spy hopping as they looked around for the source of the unpleasant noise.

What they saw terrified them. The chase boat was roaring toward them, trying to herd them deeper into the net. To confuse and frighten the whales, the men aboard the chase boat banged its hull with their hands and sticks of wood. Meanwhile the large brown trawler lumbered across the bay, pulling the net closed.

Sensing they were in danger, the pod of whales sped quickly toward the safety of the open ocean. It was a race now. Could the whales get out of the bay before the trawler pulled the net closed? The whales kicked their mighty tails as hard as they could. Ahead through the clear water, they could see the hull of the trawler crossing in front of them as it pulled the net tighter.

There was still a small opening in the net and

beyond it, the open ocean. The lead whale swam through. Then the second, third, fourth, and fifth before the net shut behind them.

Outside the bay, the whales rejoiced in their freedom. They gathered together and spy hopped, poking their massive heads out of the water and looking around to make sure they had all escaped.

Then they heard a long, mournful squeal. Trapped inside the net, Three Spots slowly circled as he searched in vain for a way out. But there was no way around the nets. Three Spots had been caught.

2
Six Months Later

On the busy city sidewalk not far from the ocean, a slender boy wandered through the crowds of people. His shaggy brown hair fell down over his forehead. The knees of his dirty jeans were torn, and the tails of his faded red flannel shirt hung out. On his back, he carried a battered, old day pack that a kid might wear on his way to school.

But it had been a long time since he'd been in school. His name was Jesse and he was eleven years old.

As Jesse looked up at the faces of the well-dressed men and women on their way home after work, his stomach growled painfully. He hadn't had a thing to eat since the day before. Suddenly he saw an older woman wearing a blue dress and carrying a fancy leather briefcase. She looked as if she probably had a couple of kids at home.

"Uh, excuse me, ma'am," Jesse said, standing in her path. "My mom dropped me off on her way

5

to work and forgot to give me bus fare back home. Can I borrow some money?"

The woman stopped and stared at him. Jesse knew she probably didn't believe his story, but it didn't matter. How could any mother not help a slight, brown-haired, brown-eyed boy of eleven?

Just as Jesse hoped, she opened her purse and gave him some change, then hurried on.

"Gee, thanks a lot," Jesse called after her. "You have a nice day."

Jesse turned and saw his buddy Perry working the crowd. Perry was older and had straight black hair that sometimes fell into his eyes. His clothes were dirty and tattered. At 14, he was taller than Jesse and more mature-looking. Like Jesse, he lived on the streets, sleeping under the highway at night and begging for money and food during the day. Jesse watched as he fell into step next to a man in a suit.

"Uh, excuse me, mister, I need to get home — " Perry began.

"Get outta here," the man growled. "I've heard that one before."

Perry stopped and muttered something under his breath. The two boys looked at each other. Jesse shrugged. Another woman was walking toward him.

"Uh, excuse me," Jesse said. "I hate to do this, but my friend and I are having a problem. We spent all our money at the Natural History Museum and we have to take the ferry back home. Could you help?"

Like the previous woman, this one opened her purse and gave him some change.

"Thank you, ma'am," Jesse said. "Thank you very much."

"You're lucky you look so young," Perry said to Jesse as the woman hurried away to catch a bus. "That's why they give you the money."

Although Jesse's empty stomach hurt, he smiled proudly. Now, through the crowd, he saw two more street kids. One was a girl named Gwenie who had long straight brown hair and was about Perry's age. The other was a kid named Vector who was a year older than Jesse. Like Perry and Jesse, their clothes were tattered and dirty.

"How'd you guys do?" Perry asked as they stood together on the sidewalk.

Gwenie shrugged. "Not so good. How about you?"

"Lousy," Perry said. "But Jesse did okay."

"Let's count up," Jesse said. Everyone handed him their change and he counted it. "Darn. It's only a couple of bucks."

"Man, we can't all eat for that," Vector groaned.

"And I need some food bad," Perry complained.

"Well, let's see what we can get," Gwenie said.

The money was only enough for one hamburger, which they divided four ways. As they left the hamburger place, they were all still hungry. Back on the sidewalk, Perry stopped and pointed.

"Hey, look," he whispered.

Ahead was a restaurant with outdoor tables behind a low wooden fence. Two couples were just rising from their seats, leaving their unfinished meals behind. In a flash, Perry and Jesse climbed over the fence and moved through the tables grabbing rolls from bread baskets and the unfinished parts of sandwiches.

As Jesse collected the food, he felt eyes upon him. He looked up and saw a man and his wife and son staring at him from another table. The boy looked about Jesse's age, but it was the mother Jesse stared at. She had long, curly blonde hair and blue eyes. She reminded Jesse of his own mother. . . .

"Hey, Jesse! Look out!" Perry shouted.

Jesse spun around just in time to see a waiter coming after him. Perry, Gwenie, and Vector were already running. Jesse quickly vaulted over the fence and back onto the sidewalk, then skillfully wove in and out of the crowd.

After half a block, the waiter gave up the chase. Jesse met up with his friends again on a corner a few blocks away, and the four of them divided up the food.

"What's with you?" Perry asked Jesse. They were sitting with their backs against a brick wall, chewing hungrily on the rolls. "You almost let that waiter nail you."

"Yeah," said Vector. "It looked like you were staring at those people with the kid. You know them or something?"

"No." Jesse shook his head and stared off at the traffic. He would never tell them that the woman reminded him of his mother. He wouldn't even tell Perry, who was his closest pal.

"I'm still starved," Perry said after he finished his share of the food.

"Me, too," said Gwenie. The group of kids stood up.

"Hey, what's that?" Vector pointed across the street. On a wide wooden pier that extended into the harbor, a crowd of people had stopped outside a group of stalls. In the stalls, men wearing stained white aprons worked feverishly while a man in a brown sports jacket ordered fish from a list in his hand.

"Half a dozen salmon," he shouted. In a stall nearby, a burly man in a white apron reached down toward a bed of crushed ice and lifted a large silver fish by the tail. As Jesse and the others watched, amazed, he threw the salmon almost twenty feet to another man who caught it and quickly wrapped it in newspaper.

"It's just an outdoor fish market," Perry said.

"Yeah, come on," Gwenie said, pulling Jesse by

the sleeve. "I may be starving, but there's no way I'm gonna eat a raw fish."

As evening descended, the hungry band of kids searched garbage cans for food, but barely found anything edible.

"This just isn't our day," Perry grumbled as he walked along the sidewalk, picking a few kernels of popcorn from a crushed box of Cracker Jack he found.

"Hey, wait!" Jesse stopped and pointed across the street. A gray van with its back door open was parked in front of a store called Cousins Catering Service. As the kids watched, a man came out of the store carrying a large rectangular white box. He put it in the back of the van and then went back into the store.

"There's a cake in that box," Gwenie whispered.

"How do you know?" Perry whispered back.

"My mom used to work in a bakery," Gwenie said.

The idea of a cake inside the box was too tempting for Jesse to resist. He dashed across the street, reached into the van, grabbed the box, and ran.

"All right!" Vector shouted with delight as he and the others followed.

3

As darkness fell, the four street kids sat under the highway near the harbor. The sky had grown gray with thick clouds during the afternoon, and it looked as if it might rain. Above them, cars raced by on the highway, creating a steady roar and filling the air with exhaust fumes. But the kids were too hungry to notice as they wolfed down pieces of the cake. It was covered with sweet white icing and had layers of yellow cake and chocolate cream filling inside.

"This is great!" Gwenie gasped, the sides of her mouth smeared white.

"Yeah," said Perry as he licked the icing off his fingers. "It's a lot better than the garbage they used to feed us at Cooperton."

Vector looked up at him with wide eyes. Cooperton was the state detention facility for runaways. "You've been there?"

"More than once," Perry said proudly. "Jesse, too."

"The first time I went there it was so bad," Gwenie said. "My mom just dumped me and then left for Houston. I don't care, I hate her anyway."

Jesse stared at her. "But you still want to see her again, right?"

Gwenie shook her head. "I don't care if I never see her again."

Jesse looked down at the flattened beer cans and loose sheets of newspaper scattered on the ground. His mother had left him, too, but it wasn't because she didn't want him around. She just had to get her act together and take care of a few things.

"So how'd you get out of Cooperton?" Vector asked Gwenie.

"I had to wait until some stupid foster home losers took me," Gwenie said. "Then I slipped."

"How come you didn't stay in the foster home?" Vector asked.

"You serious?" Jesse said. "The whole foster thing is just a scam. Foster parents are only in it for the money. The state pays them to take you into their homes."

Jesse himself had been all set to get some foster parents when he and Perry split from Cooperton. The last thing in the world he needed was some strangers pretending they were his parents and telling him what to do.

"Is that how you and Perry got out of Cooperton?" Vector asked. "By hooking up with foster parents?"

"Naw, I bolted," Jesse said.

"You bolted from Cooperton?" Vector said in disbelief. "Bull."

"I did, bonehead," Jesse said.

"Me, too," said Perry. "Three days ago."

"If they catch you, Juvenile Hall's the next stop," Vector said. "I've heard really bad things about that place."

While Cooperton was just for runaways and abandoned kids, Juvenile Hall was for kids who'd broken the law. Jesse glanced at Perry and asked if he knew anything about the place.

"I wouldn't know," Perry said with a shrug.

"So you guys are wanted," Vector said in awe.

Jesse shrugged. "Sort of." Not that anybody *really* wanted them. . . .

Above them the highway lamps went on, bathing them in yellow light. Cars raced by and the air smelled smoky, but the kids continued eating the cake. After a while the sweetness got to Jesse, but it was good to feel full for once. Next to him, Gwenie wiped her mouth with her sleeve.

"Some day I'm gonna be rich with a couple of yachts and horses," she said.

"Horses on yachts?" Jesse asked with a raised eyebrow.

"Yeah," Gwenie continued with her fantasy.

"And a family and diamonds and stuff."

Jesse had heard so many street kids talk about dreams like that . . . dreams that could never come true. He thought his dreams were a lot more realistic.

"I just want my own place," he said. "Like an apartment or something."

"You and me," Perry said, nudging him. "We'll hook up with someone. With my brains and your cute looks we're gonna be rich."

Vector laughed. Gwenie asked, "How are you gonna get rich?"

"Don't worry," Perry said. "I got a plan."

Jesse just smiled to himself. Every street kid he knew had a plan, but it always came down to the same thing — finding your next meal and a warm, dry place to spend the night. He took a deep breath of cool moist air. It felt as if it might rain.

"Whoop, whoop, whoop!" The sudden blast of a police siren split the night as headlights approached.

"Cops!" Perry shouted, jumping up. In a flash, the kids were running under the highway. They tried to lose the pursuing police car by dodging in and out of the huge graffiti-covered concrete columns that supported the overpass.

"Split up!" Perry shouted.

Running as fast as he could, Jesse headed toward the harbor and started following the street

14

that bordered the seawall. As he ran through the dark, he could hear the sounds of waves sloshing against the seawall and the distant clang of a ship's bell. But most of his attention was focused on the police sirens behind him.

"Dude!" someone called.

Jesse looked around and saw Perry waving at him from the shadows. A moment later they were running together along the seawall. The street curved and they found themselves facing a tall wooden fence covered with the scrawlings of a dozen graffiti artists.

"Dead end," Jesse muttered.

In the background, they could hear the police siren growing louder. In another couple of seconds, the cop car would come around the corner.

"What are we gonna do?" Perry gasped.

Jesse looked at the seawall. Could they scale it? It didn't matter because on the other side there was nothing but water. He turned and looked at the fence.

"Hey!" he shouted. "No problem!"

Jesse quickly crouched down and pried up a loose board in the fence, giving him and Perry just enough room to squeeze through. By the time the police car skidded around the corner, there was no sign of the boys.

Jesse and Perry stood on the other side of the fence, peering into the darkness in front of them. They could see the silhouettes of snack stands and rides and a round building that looked like a small stadium.

"What is this?" Jesse asked.

"Looks like an amusement park or something," Perry said.

The wind was picking up and whistling past them, carrying dirty candy wrappers and loose sheets of paper. Lightning flashed and they were startled by a boom of thunder. A few large drops of rain hurtled down through the stormy night sky.

"We better find someplace quick," Jesse said. He and Perry walked toward the round building and started trying the doors, but they were all locked.

"I'm gonna try down here," Jesse said, stepping down some squeaky metal stairs in the dark. The first two doors he tried were locked, but the third opened.

"Hey, Perry!" he whispered. "Down here!" A moment later Perry came down the stairs. Jesse pushed open the door and they stepped slowly into a dimly lit room.

Neither noticed the silent alarm sensor that began flashing on and off on the wall behind them.

"Must be some kind of maintenance room," Perry whispered as they looked around. The walls were lined with shelves filled with cans of cleanser and rolls of paper towels. "Hey, check it, man!"

Jesse watched as Perry found a can of spray

16

paint and began spray-painting graffiti on the maintenance room door. "Here you go, dude." Perry tossed him a can and Jesse began to paint the letter J in different shapes and sizes.

Perry pushed open the door and started to paint in the dark cinder-block-lined corridor. Jesse stayed in the maintenance room, building up his Js and adding legs and arms to them. He wasn't certain how long he had worked on them, but suddenly he realized he couldn't hear Perry anymore.

"Perry?" Jesse stepped out into the corridor and looked around. It was almost pitch-dark. Jesse took a tentative step and reached out toward the wall to his right. He could hear a weird sound, like water sloshing nearby. His fingers felt something cold, glassy, and covered with wet condensation. It felt like the inside of a refrigerator on a hot day.

Suddenly there was a burst of lightning from above. Everything lit up and Jesse found himself face-to-face with a huge black-headed monster with an enormous pink tongue and a mouthful of thick pointed teeth the size of his thumbs.

"*AHHHHH!*" Jesse felt the air rush out of his lungs as the scream tore through his throat. The next thing he knew, he was running as hard as he could down the concrete corridor. He had no idea what the thing he'd just seen was and he didn't care. He just wanted to get out of there.

17

Ahead he could see a bare light bulb in the ceiling, lighting the corridor. Jesse stopped under the bulb and caught his breath. As he looked around, he saw that the wall to his right was made of thick glass covered with a million drops of condensation. Now he knew where the sloshing sounds had come from. Behind the glass was a huge open tank of greenish water. And now he became aware of something else — a strange, distant eerie sound — high-pitched, like a whistle or squeal or some kind of bird call.

Jesse stepped toward the glass and wiped away the condensation with his palm. Cupping his hands against the glass, he tried to look in. All he could see was the dark, murky green water, but the eerie whistling sound was growing louder. Lightning crackled above and for a moment the tank was illuminated. Jesse thought he saw the shadow of something large moving toward him in the water.

As the shadow grew larger, Jesse stepped back from the glass. A moment later a huge black creature came into view. Jesse realized its head was what he'd seen in the first burst of lightning. Now, as the creature glided past, it looked at Jesse through an almond-shaped blue eye in the side of its head. Then it rolled sideways, revealing to Jesse a snow-white underbelly blemished only by three dark spots near the jaw.

Jesse stared, transfixed. He'd never been so

close to anything so massive, so beautiful, so awesome.

When the alarm bell rang in his cottage on the Northwest Adventure Park grounds, Randolph groaned and pushed himself out of bed. The park's caretaker was a Native American in his fifties and on cold, rainy nights like this, his joints felt stiff and achy. The last thing he wanted to do was get out of bed.

Rain was pelting the windows of his cottage and he could hear the wind's whistle. He had a pretty good idea of who'd tripped the alarm. It was most likely street people again, looking for a place to spend the night. *Too bad*, he thought as he ambled over to the phone and dialed the police.

A few minutes later, wearing a surfer T-shirt, jeans, and a Seattle Mariners baseball cap with rainwater dripping from the brim, Randolph unlocked the chain-link fence at the entrance to the park to allow two police cars inside.

The cop driving the first car rolled down his window. "What's up?"

"Probably some bums looking to get out of the rain," Randolph said.

The cop in the car nodded. "We've been chasing a bunch of them all night." He rolled up his window and drove into the park.

Randolph watched as four officers got out of the two cars and started to search with bright flash-

19

lights and nightsticks drawn. The caretaker didn't particularly mind letting a few homeless people stay out of the rain, but it was his job to take care of the park and sometimes the homeless did cause damage.

Not far away, in the corridor beside the tank, Jesse was still staring into the clear green waters. The creature — Jesse guessed it was a giant shark or something — swam by twice. He was waiting for it to come by again when he suddenly heard a shout echoing from somewhere beyond the corridor.

"Jesse! Run!" It was Perry warning him.

Jesse turned and pulled open the nearest door. Flash! Instantly he was blinded by the bright beams of the cops' flashlights. Jesse quickly turned away to run, but he tripped over a trash can and fell hard, scraping his elbows and knees against the cold, rough concrete floor.

Jumping again to his feet, Jesse caught sight of an EXIT sign at the top of the stairs and started to climb up. Outside he could hear the roar of pouring rain. Just as he reached the top, a heavy hand came down on his shoulder. Jesse spun around, expecting to see a cop, but instead he looked up into the dark wrinkled face of a man wearing a baseball cap and surfing T-shirt. They grappled for a second at the top of the stairs. Feeling the man grab onto his backpack, Jesse instantly slid his arms out of the straps, leaving Randolph with nothing but the pack in his hands.

Jesse spun around and darted away out into the pouring rain . . . *Wham!* Right into the hands of a waiting cop.

4

The offices of the city's Department of Youth Services were painted a dull olive-green, probably with camouflage paint left over from World War II. The walls were lined with dusty plants atop battered old filing cabinets. At a dozen gray metal desks scattered around the room, harried-looking people spoke on the phone and typed reports.

Jesse sat beside one desk, watching sullenly as a burly social worker named Dwight read through his arrest record. Dwight had a mustache and was wearing faded blue jeans and a white button-down shirt with the sleeves rolled up. Jesse had known him for a long time.

"Let's see," Dwight said, scanning the rap sheet. "Breaking and entering. Malicious mischief. Vandalism. Resisting arrest . . ." He raised an eyebrow toward Jesse. "Anything else I should know about?"

"I robbed a few banks," Jesse said with a shrug. "Is that a problem?"

Dwight smiled, knowing Jesse was pulling his leg.

"It's a good thing you were only out of Cooperton three days," the social worker said with a wink.

Jesse smirked. "You miss me, Dwight?"

"Perry split Cooperton with you," Dwight said, ignoring the question. "Was he with you at that adventure park?"

"Perry who?" Jesse asked innocently.

"There were two graffiti jobs on the wall," Dwight said, growing annoyed and pointing at Jesse's paint-stained hands. "One was yours. Who did the other?"

"Don't know," Jesse said with a shrug. He wasn't about to rat on Perry.

"Listen to me, Jesse," Dwight said, leaning close. "You're a cut above Perry. You're young. You still have a chance to save yourself. You should stay away from that kid. Perry's been on the street too long. He's a lost cause."

"Perry who?" Jesse asked again.

Dwight looked mad. He didn't like it when Jesse played games with him. It frustrated Dwight that so many kids like Jesse were on the verge of throwing their lives away, and were either too young to know it, or simply didn't care.

"Okay, Jesse," he growled. "I just spent forty-five minutes on a conference call between the police department and that adventure park trying to get them to drop the charges. And you know what? You're lucky because we made a deal. The cops have a standing file on you now, but they'll throw it away, if . . ."

"Sure, there's always an if," Jesse said sullenly. "What's the big if this time?"

"If you clean up the mess you made," Dwight said. "You got fifteen days, eight hours a day. You have a problem with that?"

"Yeah." Jesse gave him a big nod. "Why should I clean up anything?"

Dwight looked disgusted. "I just did you a big favor by keeping you out of Juvenile Hall, Jesse. The least you could do is show some appreciation." But Jesse just shrugged. Dwight shook his head. "Boy, I don't know why I work overtime on you."

" 'Cause you like my looks?" Jesse asked.

"Okay, this is it," Dwight snapped, pointing an angry finger at him. "You mess up again and I am out of the picture. Next time it's definitely Juvenile Hall for you. Your friend Perry tell you how bad it gets in Juvenile Hall?"

Jesse shook his head, but inside he was surprised. Perry had pretended he'd never been there.

"Well, I hope you never get to ask him," Dwight

said. He took a deep breath and settled down, then flipped open another file. "Okay, now here's the rest of the deal, Jesse. Your placement with the Greenwoods is still okay. You're lucky they've already met you and like you. They're a nice foster family and they don't care about this . . . incident."

"Oh, yeah?" Jesse pretended to be surprised. "What's wrong with *them*?"

"I get it," Dwight said. "Because they want you in their home, there's something wrong with them?"

"What do you think?" Jesse asked with a smirk.

"Let me explain something you obviously don't understand," Dwight said. "You're still real young, Jesse. At least on paper you look that way. So people are willing to give you a few more chances. Not an infinite number, but a few. Get it?"

Jesse just shrugged. It didn't matter to him whether he had one chance or a million. Sooner or later he knew he'd be back on the street.

"Got any questions about this?" Dwight asked, holding up the foster file.

"Yeah," Jesse said. "You hear from my mom?"

Dwight looked surprised, then sighed and shook his head. "You still want me to hear from your mom?"

So he hasn't heard, Jesse thought. "I just want to know if she's okay," he said.

Dwight nodded slowly. The anger seemed to have gone. "Look, Jesse, nobody's heard from your mom in six years."

Jesse looked down at the scuffed gray tiles on the floor. He wanted to believe his mom was out there somewhere and she still cared about him. She was just trying to set things up nice before she came for him.

"Hey, Jesse, I got something for you." Dwight reached behind his chair and handed him his beat-up backpack. Jesse quickly reached out and pulled it on, glad to have it again. Across the desk, Dwight stood up.

"Okay, kid, the Greenwoods are waiting for you," he said. "Let's go."

On the bridge over the harbor, Jesse looked out the window of Dwight's car. The sun was just starting to turn orange over the ocean to the west. Below them the harbor was filled with tankers and ships.

"We'll be at the Greenwoods' in about ten minutes," Dwight said as he drove. "You nervous?"

Jesse shook his head. He didn't care enough to be nervous. Next to him, Dwight smiled slightly.

"Well, I'm nervous," he said. "I bet the Greenwoods are probably nervous. I'm glad someone's not nervous."

Soon they turned down a road and into a community of two-story wooden houses.

"That's their place," Dwight said.

Ahead Jesse saw a dark green house with white trim and a neatly cut front lawn. A dark-haired man wearing jeans and a green workshirt with a name tag over the pocket was out in the driveway, standing near a light blue tow truck with GREEN-WOOD AUTO REPAIR painted on the side. Jesse recognized him as Glen, the man who'd come to see him while he was still in Cooperton.

"In case you forgot," Dwight said. "Glen Greenwood owns an auto repair shop."

Jesse just shrugged. The truth was he had forgotten.

A second later they pulled into the driveway. Glen Greenwood started to saunter toward Dwight's car. Before he got there, a woman wearing jeans and a light blue blouse came out of the house and ran down the porch steps, smiling and waving. She had long, wavy blonde hair and big brown eyes. Jesse remembered her, too. Her name was Annie.

"Hi, Jesse," Annie called. "Nice to see you again."

The only reason Jesse got out of the car was because Dwight nudged him. He hugged his pack tightly to his chest and stared at the ground with nothing to say. Dwight and the Greenwoods said hello. Then Glen turned to Jesse.

"Got any stuff to bring in?" he asked.

Jesse shook his head.

"He's traveling pretty light these days," Dwight said.

"That's the way," Glen said. "Nothing slowing him down."

Jesse hated it when adults tried to act cool. It just made them seem like a bunch of dorks.

"Well, Jesse," Annie said, "why don't we go inside and have dinner?"

Jesse reluctantly followed Annie inside. Meanwhile, Dwight went back to his car and got out the foster parent agreements for Glen to sign.

"Always have to have some paperwork," Dwight said, handing the papers on a clipboard to Glen. "I bought a car the other day. With the loan and everything I had to fill out thirty-seven pages."

Glen nodded and signed in the appropriate places. "I look at this more like a lease," he said. "We're not quite ready to buy, if you know what I mean."

Dwight nodded. He understood. Especially with a kid like Jesse.

At dinnertime, Jesse sat uncomfortably at the round, wooden kitchen table while Glen set out the dishes. Annie was at the stove, taking dinner out. Everyone was acting nervous and stilted. Jesse felt as if he should probably try to make conversation. He looked around and noticed something unusual.

"How come you have a computer in the kitchen?" he asked.

"Weird, isn't it?" Glen said.

"I write on it," Annie said.

"I fixed her up an office to write in," Glen said. "But she won't use it."

"I work better in the kitchen," Annie said. "Maybe it's because I used to do my homework at the kitchen table. An office just seems too intimidating."

"You write books and stuff?" Jesse asked.

"No, I'm a teacher," Annie said. "But since I have the summer off, I decided to try to be a journalist. So far I've just sold a couple of stories."

"No one's paid her yet," Glen said, sitting down and offering a platter of chicken to Jesse. "Go ahead, dig in."

Jesse took a piece in his hands and bit into it.

"One of the stories I did was about you kids at Cooperton," Annie said. "That's how I met Dwight."

Jesse nodded. He sort of remembered the story now. She'd done the article and thought Cooperton was pretty bad. So she decided to try being a foster parent.

It was quiet for a few moments. Then Glen cleared his throat.

"So what kinds of things are you interested in, Jesse?" he asked.

"Uh . . . nothing really," Jesse said, biting hungrily into a drumstick. It got quiet again. Jesse noticed that Glen and Annie had both stopped eating and were staring at him with puzzled looks. Suddenly Annie jumped up.

"So, hey, what do you want to drink with dinner, Jesse?" she asked. "Juice, milk?"

"Coffee," Jesse replied. "Black with tons of sugar."

Again Glen and Annie looked puzzled. Jesse wondered what the problem was. But Annie quickly put a pot on the stove, and pretty soon he had a steaming cup of black coffee.

Later they showed him his bedroom. It was kind of small and cozy and they'd put up a map of the United States and some posters of baseball players Jesse had never heard of. On the bed was a small white box.

"It's a little present," Annie said. "Go ahead and open it."

Jesse eyed the box suspiciously. It was bad enough that the Greenwoods were his foster parents now, but he felt really uncomfortable with them giving him presents. Glen must have sensed his discomfort because he took the box away and put it on the shelf.

"Maybe later," he said.

Jesse wished they'd both just leave him alone, but instead, Annie went to the wooden dresser and took out a new blue shirt. "I bought you some clothes, Jesse. Dwight says your favorite color is blue."

Jesse shrugged. He wasn't sure what his favorite color was. Annie looked worried.

"Dwight told me you wrote that on the form," she said.

Jesse nodded. He remembered that they'd made him fill out a form. Half the time he hadn't known what to write so he'd just made things up.

"Well, we can always exchange them if you want," Annie said. Another one of those awkward silences followed. Jesse fiddled with a clock radio near the bed and found a rap station.

"I couldn't live a night without a radio when I was your age," Annie said.

It was hard for Jesse to believe that she'd *ever* been his age. He turned the music up and wished the Greenwoods would go away and leave him alone.

"Uh, we'll get out of here and let you hit the sack," Glen said. "If you need anything, we're right downstairs."

"The bathroom's at the end of the hall," Annie added.

Finally they left. Jesse let out a big sigh of relief. He turned off the radio and walked over to the window to look out into the dark. Suddenly the door opened again, startling him. He spun around and saw that Annie had stuck her head in.

"I just wanted to say we're glad to have you here, Jesse. Good night."

The door closed again. Jesse turned toward the window and looked out at the yard. Beyond that, he could see rooftops and then the bridge to the city all lit up. He imagined Perry and Gwenie and Vector out on the streets. Jesse turned away from the window, shaking his head. What was he doing in this house with these weird people? He didn't know. But at least he'd have a warm, dry place to spend the night. He walked back to the light switch and turned it off, then took his harmonica out of his pack, sat down on the floor, and started playing softly in the dark.

Downstairs, Annie and Glen were sitting quietly at the kitchen table when they heard the harmonica. Dwight hadn't said anything about Jesse playing an instrument. They looked at each other with wonder. Jesse, their new foster son, was full of surprises.

5

The next day Jesse sat in the passenger seat of Glen's tow truck as they pulled up to the Northwest Adventure Park. In the daylight, Jesse was surprised at how rundown the place looked. The fences were brown with rust, the signs were faded and peeling. Loose paper and candy wrappers littered the ground. They got out of the truck and Glen took an old bike out of the back and set it down on the ground for Jesse. A white plastic basket hung from the handlebars.

"You remember the turn just before the bridge?" Glen asked. "That was Burns Road. My auto repair shop is straight up from there. If you go another six blocks, you get to our house, got that?"

Jesse nodded and grabbed the bike's handlebars.

"And Jesse," Glen continued. "When you get into the park, ask for a guy named Randolph, okay?"

Again Jesse nodded. Without a word he pushed the bike toward the park's entrance. Behind him Glen watched with his hands on his hips, wondering if the kid would ever start talking to him.

Inside the park, Jesse rode past the Ferris wheel and the carousel. Ahead of him was the amphitheater, the round building with the big water tank where Jesse had seen that big shark or whatever it was.

When Jesse asked for Randolph, a worker pointed him toward a small, white cottage on stilts near the harbor side of the park. Jesse climbed the stairs and peeked inside. The cottage was lined with raw yellowed wood. There were Indian rugs on the floor and lots of books on the shelves. Jesse noticed swimming flippers, a mask, and an old black and red wet suit hanging on a hook.

He tried knocking, but no one answered. Finally Jesse decided to wait inside for this Randolph dude. He pulled open the door. The cottage smelled of freshly burned wood and Jesse noticed a large collection of carved miniature totem poles and bears and whales on the tables and shelves.

Then he heard the door close behind him and spun around. Jesse was stunned to see who was standing there. It was the Indian guy who'd pulled off his backpack the night he got caught by the cops. Today he was wearing a plaid shirt and his long hair was pulled back into a ponytail.

For a moment, the two of them just stared at each other.

"You're Randolph?" Jesse asked.

The older man smiled, revealing crooked yellow teeth. "Well, the artist returns. Welcome back."

Randolph wasted no time putting Jesse to work. Lugging a plastic yellow pail of paint solvent, a box of steel wool, and heavy black rubber gloves, the caretaker led Jesse back to the corridor beside the tank.

"This is the underwater observation room," Randolph said. "I imagine it looks familiar."

Jesse smiled sheepishly at the dumb-looking stick figures he and Perry had painted on the walls and large thick windows. Even a sign next to the tank that said WINDOW TO THE SEA was covered with graffiti.

"We're all great admirers of your art around here," Randolph said, setting down the bucket and handing the gloves to Jesse. "But all good things must come to an end. It is now time to let your creativity flow backward."

This guy is weird, Jesse thought as he slipped the rubber gloves on.

"You know what to do?" Randolph asked.

Jesse nodded and picked up a wad of steel wool. Dipping it into the solvent, he started to scrub the spray paint off the wall.

The work was tedious and boring. After only

ten minutes, Jesse had already started to day-dream about taking off. The problem was that Dwight said the next time he bolted, they'd send him to Juvenile Hall. It sounded like a real bummer. Jesse figured it might be better to wait until he had someplace good to go and then split.

Jesse worked with his back toward the observation windows. The water inside was calm when he started, but suddenly he heard a whooshing, splashing sound. He turned around and saw that the water was churning, leaving bubbles of air swirling against the glass.

He turned and scrubbed some more. A few moments later he was aware of the approaching sound again. This time he turned in time to see that huge fish with the three white spots under his jaw glide by. Jesse had never seen anything so big. Curious to get a better look at it, he dropped the steel wool in the bucket and started walking along the side of the tank.

The fish was nowhere in sight. Where was it?

Jesse came to a stairway and climbed up. The stairs led to a platform that extended into the tank. Behind the platform was a wooden wall with NORTHWEST ADVENTURE PARK carved into it, and a large model of a lighthouse. Across the tank from the platform were long rows of concrete seats where people sat to watch the shows. Overhead the sky was blue and dotted with small clouds shaped like cotton balls. Jesse shielded his eyes from the sunlight that glinted off the tank's surface. Maybe he could see the thing from the platform. He ducked under a chain and walked until he was leaning against the railing that prevented him from falling into the water. The creature had to be here somewhere. Jesse stared down into the water. Sunlight glinting off the rippling surface made him squint.

Suddenly there was an explosion in the middle of the tank as the huge fish shot straight up out of the water like a missile and then crashed back down with a huge splash that sent a shower of spray in every direction. Jesse stood there wide-eyed. He'd never seen anything like it.

Whap! A hand slammed down on his shoulder, startling him. Jesse spun around and came face-to-face with Randolph.

"What are you doing here?" the caretaker asked angrily.

"Nothing." Jesse tried to shake his shoulder free.

Across the choppy water of the tank, the huge fish surfaced, blowing a great gasp of spray and mist from its blowhole. Jesse stared at it.

"Killer whale," Randolph said. "Over seven thousand pounds. Enough power in those jaws to crush bones into oatmeal. His name's Willy and he gets into moods. You always have to give him his space. Know what I mean?"

Across the tank, Willy made a long, high-pitched whistling squeal. Jesse recognized it as the sound he'd heard the night he was spray-painting. He stared, awestruck as Willy flapped his powerful tail and shot forward into the water.

"Don't bother him, and he won't bother you, understand?" Randolph said.

"Sure," Jesse replied, although he really wasn't certain what the caretaker meant. The next thing he knew, Randolph was leading him back to the underwater observation room to continue cleaning the graffiti.

As the day progressed, small crowds of people started to come in to see the show in the amphitheater. Downstairs, Jesse had never worked so long or so hard at one job in his whole life. He was certain that he would have bolted by now, were it not for that whale, Willy. It was weird, but there was something about Willy that made him want to stick around.

Outside in the amphitheater, Jesse could hear music and a smattering of applause. It sounded as if there was a show going on. He decided to take a break and go see.

The theater was practically empty. Sitting here and there on the long rows of concrete seats, a few dozen people were watching a woman in a bright orange-and-white wet suit who stood on the platform beside the tank. On the front of her wet suit was a small emblem of a killer whale.

She had short brown hair and spoke energetically into a microphone around her neck. In the water, a pair of sea lions were doing back flips, grabbing small fish out of her hands as they jumped.

"As you can see," the young woman told the crowd, "Olivia and Belinda flip out at lunchtime. . . . Let's hear a big round of applause for Olivia and Belinda."

A couple of people clapped, and everyone began to file out of the amphitheater.

"Don't forget, ladies and gentlemen," the woman said with forced cheer, "in a couple of minutes you'll be able to have a look at Willy, our prize orca whale, right here in the main tank."

The spectators kept filing out. Jesse watched the woman shrug and walk away with the sea lions following. On the other side of the main tank was a holding tank and Jesse saw two workmen raise a barricade. Willy, the big black-and-white whale, was in the holding tank. Jesse was surprised that Willy didn't swim out into the larger tank until the workmen prodded him with poles to get him to go.

A moment later, Jesse was distracted by the sounds of a heated argument. He turned and saw the woman in the orange-and-white wet suit talking to two men. One of the men wore sunglasses and a dark suit. His hair was slicked back like a movie star. The other man was heavy and had a red face. He was wearing khaki slacks and a blue-

and-white-striped short-sleeved shirt. It seemed to Jesse that they were arguing about Willy.

"Look, Dial," the woman said to the slick-looking man in the suit, "you can come down and glare all you want, but that's not going to change a darn thing!"

"You just don't understand, Rae," Dial replied. "This isn't some personal project."

"I realize that," Rae snapped back at him.

"The problem is, we're not seeing any progress here," the heavy man said. "We need that whale in the show."

"You don't have to tell me that, Wade," Rae replied.

Jesse turned back to the tank and looked for Willy. He spotted the whale pressing his head against the far wall of the tank, as if he were hiding. Obviously, there was some kind of problem concerning Willy and no one, including Willy, seemed very happy about it. Jesse turned back and looked at the woman talking to the men. She looked younger than they were, and quite pretty. She lowered her voice and Jesse could no longer hear what she was saying, but he was impressed with how she stood up to them.

He looked for Willy again, but the whale was gone. Jesse scowled and leaned over the tank, searching for him. Suddenly Willy rocketed straight up in front of him and came down with a giant splash. Jesse jumped back, and nearly

40

knocked over the woman named Rae, who had just left the men. They both turned and stared at each other. The look of surprise on Rae's face turned hard.

"You're the kid who likes to paint, right?" she said.

"I guess." Jesse shrugged. He hated that accusing tone of voice, even when he *had* done something wrong.

"You really messed up our observation area," Rae said. "That makes me mad. We have enough problems around here without a graffiti attitude."

"Sorry," Jesse snapped angrily. He didn't need her lecturing him.

Rae gave him a skeptical look. "Really?"

Jesse shook his head.

Rae cracked a smile. "That's what I thought."

Jesse turned back and looked at the tank. Willy was floating nearby. It seemed to Jesse that the whale was watching them.

"You like whales?" Rae asked.

"I like *him*," Jesse said.

"Well, he doesn't like anybody," Rae said. "You better be careful around him. Willy's a very special case."

"So who isn't?" Jesse asked.

Rae studied him for a moment more. "Listen, this isn't a show, okay. I know you've got work to do."

41

6

The days passed. Each morning Jesse rode his bike to the adventure park and scrubbed the graffiti off the wall of the underwater observation room. Each evening he rode back to the Greenwoods' house. So far the Greenwoods had been okay. They hadn't made any demands on him, and they were always careful to be polite and nice. But Jesse doubted it could last much longer.

One evening after getting home, Jesse sat with his back against the fence in the backyard and watched the sun turn pink-orange over the ocean while he played softly on his harmonica.

Then, out of the corner of his eye, he noticed Glen strolling across the yard toward him, carrying a couple of old baseball mitts. The next thing Jesse knew, Glen tossed one of them toward him.

"Here's a baseball glove if you ever want to play catch," he said.

Jesse stared at his foster father as if he were from outer space. "Catch?"

"Sure," Glen said. "I like to throw a ball around once in a while. I've had both of these mitts since about eighth grade. Check out the sweet spot on that baby. It's grooved. I used to stay up nights spitting in it and slugging it with my fist."

Jesse stared at the mitt and imagined Glen spitting in it. This guy was just plain weird. He gazed up at him. "How much they paying you to be my jailers?"

Glen looked startled, as if someone had unexpectedly smacked him in the face. He started pacing around on the grass in front of Jesse. "Oh, sure, you're a real money-maker for us, Jesse. A real cash cow. With this foster-parenting deal and about a million dollars I ought to be able to retire when I'm a hundred."

Jesse just gave him a sullen look.

"You think Annie and I are jailers, huh?" Glen said. "Okay, well, I'm kind of new at this. Maybe you can give me a hand?"

"What?" Jesse asked, caught off guard.

"What kind of rules do you need?" Glen asked.

"You're asking me?" Jesse looked at him as if he were crazy.

"Sure," Glen said. "I figure you're the expert here."

"I don't know," Jesse said with a shrug.

"Sure you do," Glen said. "I bet with all the places you've been, you've forgotten more rules than I ever knew."

Jesse stood up and started pacing, too, imitating Glen. "Okay, let's see," he said. "The first rule is that you have to give me an allowance once a week."

"Money?" Glen pretended to look surprised.

"Yeah," Jesse said. To his amazement, Glen pulled out his wallet and handed him a five-dollar bill.

"What else?" Glen asked.

Jesse quickly pocketed the money and turned toward the house before Glen could change his mind and ask for it back. "I'll have to think about the other ones," he called over his shoulder.

"All right, but here's the deal," Glen said. Jesse stopped to listen. "How about you try to get to bed by ten, make it down for breakfast every morning, and home for dinner at seven. And no wandering around without checking in with us. We want to know where you are."

Jesse didn't reply, but he figured he might be able to do that in return for five dollars a week.

"Once we've got that straight," Glen said, "we'll figure out the real rules. Okay?"

Jesse stared back at him, looking him in the eye for the first time. "Okay," he said.

One day the following week, Jesse finished scrubbing away the graffiti. It was still morning at the park, and he slid the heavy gloves off and took out his harmonica. All week he'd been playing a little game with Willy. Standing near the thick glass observation window, he blew some notes on the harmonica and then waited. A moment later Willy rose from the bottom of the tank and passed in front of the glass, returning the sound of the harmonica with his own high-pitched squeal.

Jesse played a few more notes, but this time Willy didn't respond. Wondering if there was something on the surface distracting the whale, Jesse climbed the stairs. In the amphitheater, he saw Rae, the trainer, coming toward him. Suddenly, Willy surfaced near her and slapped the water with his tail, instantly soaking her.

"You have a nice day, too, Wilhelm!" Rae shouted angrily at the whale as she wiped the wet hair off her forehead.

Jesse walked toward Rae. He thought she was really pretty. During the course of the week he'd even gotten to like her, sort of.

"He likes messing around with everybody's head, doesn't he?" Jesse said to her.

"You get it?" Rae asked.

Jesse nodded. He thought he understood exactly what Willy was doing.

Rae shook her head. "I don't get it. Orcas are usually smart and nice. Willy's smart . . . and nasty. You really like him?"

Again, Jesse nodded.

"Well, it's too bad you have to scrub off all that graffiti," Rae said. "Maybe I could use you."

"I finished," Jesse said.

"Oh, yeah?" Rae smiled a little. "Well, come on. You can help me out."

They went down the stairs and around to the back of the amphitheater. Jesse realized they were headed toward a small wooden shack. As they came close to it, he could smell something really foul.

"What's that?" he asked.

"Rotten fish," Rae said, pushing open the door. "Welcome to the fish shack."

Inside, the smell was even worse. There was a long table and a sink along one wall. On the table was a big silver can of dead fish. Flies were buzzing all over the place and the stench was so bad it made Jesse's eyes water. He almost wanted to barf. He didn't know why he stayed. Maybe it was because he liked being near Rae, or maybe it was because he knew they were going to do something for Willy. He and Rae both put on long rubber aprons and gloves and stood at the table. Jesse watched as Rae started sorting through the dead fish.

"Every day we have to sort out what Willy can eat from the cheap junk they're buying for him," Rae said. She held up a whole fish. "See? This is good."

Jesse reached into the can and took out a nearly whole fish with a gash in its stomach. "What about this?"

Rae shook her head. "Broken belly. Toss it."

Jesse threw the fish in a garbage can. Soon their aprons were covered with blood, scales, and fish guts as they searched for the few good fish in the mess of bad ones.

"So tell me, Jesse," Rae said as they worked. "Are you really rotten, or are you just faking it?"

Instead of answering, Jesse glared at her. He didn't like people who taunted him.

"Hey," Rae said with a gentle smile. "You don't have to fight everybody, okay?"

The soft tone of her voice drained the anger out of Jesse. Besides, he had questions about Willy he hoped she could answer.

"Willy's a killer whale," he said. "Would he kill us?"

Rae shook her head. "Orcas are just hunters. They eat fish mostly. Sometimes birds, squid, seals. What Willy really likes is salmon. That's like chocolate to him."

"Does he get much salmon?" Jesse asked.

Rae looked surprised. "Are you serious? Dial and Wade would never spend that kind of money."

"Who are Dial and Wade?" Jesse asked.

"Dial's the real sharp dresser with the sunglasses. He owns this place. Wade's the heavy guy with the red face. He's the general manager."

"Maybe if they gave Willy salmon, he'd be happier and learn his tricks," Jesse said.

Rae nodded and smiled sadly. "You might be right, Jesse, but don't hold your breath."

"So what'll happen to Willy if he doesn't learn his tricks?" Jesse asked.

"Don't ask," Rae replied.

7

That night after bedtime, Jesse slipped out of the window of his room at the Greenwoods' house and rode his bike over the bridge and through the misty darkness to the adventure park.

He had finished his job at the park and he wanted to see Willy one last time. He snuck in and climbed to the edge of the main tank. It was very quiet. The surface of the tank was still and dark except for a tiny glowing streak where the moonlight came through the mist. Jesse took out his harmonica and blew a few soft notes.

A moment later Willy surfaced like a submarine, releasing a big gasp of spray through his blowhole. Jesse smiled proudly. He was the only one who could get Willy to do things like that.

Suddenly a light flashed on nearby. Through a doorway, Jesse could see the silhouette of Randolph coming toward him. Jesse knew he'd be in trouble if he got caught sneaking in, so he quietly jumped up to run. But his feet slipped! A split-second later Jesse banged his head into the side of the tank, and fell, unconscious, into the water.

Randolph didn't hear the splash or see Jesse disappear under the surface. He had turned toward another part of the amphitheater. In the tank, Jesse slowly sank toward the bottom, his legs and arms hanging loosely like some life-size doll. The only living creature who knew what had happened was Willy.

Jesse was the same size as a full-grown seal, and probably tasted equally good. Willy swam toward him with his large, pointed teeth bared.

As the huge killer whale swam closer, he realized it wasn't a seal. It was that human. He slid his head under the sinking boy, catching his body, and rose toward the surface. Still unconscious, Jesse had no idea what was happening as Willy rolled him off his back and onto the trainer's platform.

A few seconds later, Jesse woke in a spasm of coughing. He felt as if he was choking. Finally he managed to clear his lungs and get up. His head throbbed painfully and he was shocked to discover that he was soaking wet. As his teeth began to chatter in the cool air, he gazed out at the tank where Willy was slowly swimming back and forth, as if guarding him.

I must have fallen in, Jesse thought, feeling

the bump on his forehead. *Willy must have saved me!*

A little while later, Jesse sat wrapped in an Indian blanket on the sofa in Randolph's cottage. He was so cold and wet that he had no choice but to go to Randolph and tell him what had happened. To his surprise, the caretaker wasn't angry.

"You must have something special, kid," the Indian man said as he handed Jesse a steaming mug of instant coffee. "Otherwise Willy would have eaten you."

"Special?" Jesse scowled as he sipped the coffee. It felt good and warm.

"High blood," Randolph said. "Indian roots."

"No way." Jesse knew he didn't have any Indian blood.

"Then you're just one lucky little white boy," Randolph said with a grin. "You like the sound of that better?"

"Willy just doesn't have a problem with me," Jesse said with a modest shrug. "We appreciate each other."

"Appreciate?" Randolph laughed. "I'll say. He saved your butt."

"Willy's okay," Jesse said. "I don't know why everybody has such a problem with him."

"Hey, I know that whale," Randolph interrupted him. "He *does not* like visitors in his tank, understand? What were you doing there anyway?"

"Saying good-bye," Jesse admitted. Suddenly, he realized he didn't want to leave Willy. Not after the whale saved his life. "Only, I don't want to say good-bye, you know?"

Randolph nodded. Jesse noticed a small wooden carving of a killer whale on the shelf. It was painted black with white markings, just like Willy.

"You ever look into Willy's eyes?" Randolph asked. "Orcas discovered the stars before man was even a whisper on this planet. An orca can look into a man's soul if he wants. Willy won't look at Rae or me, but maybe he sees something in you."

Jesse was surprised to discover that he hoped it was true. He picked up the carving of the orca and studied it more closely.

"Want to keep that?" Randolph asked.

Jesse looked at him with surprise, and then nodded eagerly.

"Good," the caretaker said. "Now come on, I have to take you home."

Twenty minutes later Randolph pulled his old VW bus onto the Greenwoods' street. Jesse could see that all the lights in the house were on.

"Looks like your parents are still up," Randolph said.

"They're not my parents," Jesse corrected him.

"Okay, whoever they are, here they come," Randolph said.

Glen and Annie came running out the front door before the VW bus had even stopped in the driveway. Jesse could see they were upset. Annie's eyes looked red, as if she'd been crying.

"Jesse, what happened?" she asked as he got out of the van still wrapped in the blanket.

"I was at work," Jesse said.

"Snuck out of here at midnight to clean graffiti?" Glen frowned. "That's an amazing story."

Jesse just shrugged. Annie peeled back the blanket and touched his wet clothes.

"You're soaked," she gasped, puzzled.

"Fell in the tank," Jesse explained.

"The whale tank?" Glen turned and stared at Randolph. "What's going on here?"

Randolph was silent. As far as he was concerned, it was Jesse's job to explain.

"I slipped," Jesse said. "It was my fault."

Annie and Glen stared again at Randolph. The Indian caretaker took a deep breath and decided he'd better help out after all.

"Hey, folks, I'm Randolph and I've been supervising Jesse down at the park," he said. "Jesse's been doing a real good job. He finished with the graffiti and has been helping out in some other areas. He's even made some friends. The thing is, we could use him for the rest of the summer, if that's all right with you. Make a job out of it. Pay him a little something, too. What do you say?"

Jesse couldn't believe Randolph was offering him a job. Suddenly he knew he wanted it more than anything. He quickly turned and begged his foster parents. "Please let me. I really want to."

Glen studied him. "You finally found something you're into?"

Jesse nodded eagerly.

"I, uh, guess it sounds okay," Annie said a little uncertainly.

"Yeah, okay," Glen said. "But play it straight up, Jesse. Next time you want to take off at midnight, let's talk about it, okay?"

Jesse nodded again. Annie put her hands on his shoulders and led him inside. "You must be freezing. Let's get you in a hot shower."

Glen turned back to the caretaker and held out his hand. "Thanks, Randolph. You pull him out of the tank?"

"Nope," Randolph said, shaking his hand.

Glen looked puzzled. He'd seen the tank and knew the walls were too high for someone swimming in it to climb out by himself. "The whale?"

But Randolph just gave him a mysterious smile and walked back to his van. "Good night, Mr. Greenwood." He got in and drove away.

* * *

54

The next morning as Jesse walked toward the amphitheater, he noticed a large sign across the entrance that said, ATTRACTION CLOSED. He could hear loud, anguished squeals and water splashing as if a struggle were taking place. *Willy!* Jesse thought, ducking under the sign and hurrying inside.

As he neared the holding tank, he could see a bunch of people standing around it. They had Willy trapped in a net and pinned against the holding tank wall while some guy in a white jacket tried to examine him. No wonder Willy was squealing unhappily and thrashing around so much. Rae was standing nearby, talking to that heavy guy with the red face, Wade. Rae looked mad. Jesse ducked down behind a seat and tried to hear what they were arguing about.

"This examination area is totally inadequate," Rae was saying.

"Sorry, it's all we've got," Wade replied.

"Willy could hurt himself in that net," Rae said. "We've told you that seven times."

Wade turned impatiently to the man in the white jacket. "Could you finish the examination now?"

"Not yet," the man replied and continued working. Rae looked really frustrated.

"Look," she said to Wade, "you and Dial bought Willy from some slimeball whale catcher. He was too big and too old to be caught in the first place. He's *not* a natural performer. Then you put him in a tank that was built for your dolphin show. *Alone!* And you expect me to work miracles with him."

"That's right." Wade nodded vigorously. "We pay you to train Willy, not analyze him."

"Well, these were not the circumstances you described to me when I signed on for this job," Rae said angrily.

Wade glared at her. "You're a professional, right? Your job is to *make it work*."

Willy kept thrashing and squealing in the net. Jesse knew Rae was right. Willy really could hurt himself in there. While the others argued, Jesse slipped quietly toward the holding tank. He had to do something to help Willy.

Meanwhile, Rae and Wade were getting louder.

"That whale is a bottomless cash pit!" Wade was shouting. "Dial's given me a line and I'm not gonna cross it."

"This is not about cutting corners!" Rae shouted back. "Willy needs a bigger tank. Dial promised me he'd build one."

The argument had caught the attention of the men standing around the holding tank. While they watched Wade and Rae, Jesse snuck behind them and started to undo the hooks holding the net against the wall.

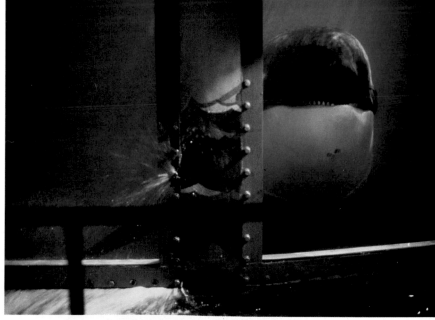

"If Willy brought in customers, we could spend more money on him!" Wade shouted back. "But since Willy isn't bringing anyone in, we have no money to spend."

Their argument was interrupted by shouts from the men around the holding tank as Willy got out of the net and glided happily into the main tank.

"Darn it!" Wade shouted.

Jesse backed away quietly, pleased that Willy was free to swim again. Suddenly, he sensed someone behind him. It was Randolph with his hair tucked under a red bandanna around his forehead.

"I saw what you did," the caretaker said.

"So?" Jesse tried to act brave, but inside he felt scared. If Randolph told Wade, Jesse knew he'd be in big trouble. But Randolph didn't seem angry.

"Nothing," Randolph said. It seemed as if he were trying to hide a smile. "I'm sure Willy is quite grateful."

Later that day, Wade stood near the main tank with Dial, the owner of the park. There were hardly any customers around as they talked quietly about Willy.

"It's the same old story," Wade said as they watched Randolph drive the forklift with a pallet of frozen fish toward the fish shack. "Willy's not performing. It's just costing us more and more money, and now Rae says we have to expand the tank."

"Oh, sure," Dial said with a mocking chuckle. "Why don't we just send him to a fancy hotel? Is this what I get for bringing this whale in to boost business? I just finished paying five thousand bucks on his last insurance premium, and now I'm supposed to spend another hundred grand to expand that psychotic orca's playpen?"

"If you ask me," Wade said, speaking in a whisper, "Willy's worth more dead than alive."

Dial nodded and muttered, "I hate that whale."

8

"Well, it's for this whale," Jesse was telling the guy at the outdoor fish market. "I don't care what it is as long as it's fresher than the junk they're feeding him now."

He'd gone to the fish market to buy Willy some fresh fish, but he was shocked at how much it cost.

"I'll see what I can do," the guy said and disappeared into his stall. A few moments later he returned with something wrapped in newspaper.

"Thanks," Jesse said. Water and fish blood dripped from the newspaper as he placed the package in the pail hanging from the handlebars of his bike and started away.

"Yo! Jesse dude!" someone shouted. Jesse recognized the voice. He looked around and saw Perry leave a bunch of older kids across the street and come toward him.

"Hey, new clothes," Perry said as Jesse walked his bike along the pier. "You got a new gig?"

"Staying with some people," Jesse replied carefully, not wanting Perry to know he was living with a foster family.

"What happened to you that night at the park?" Perry asked. "I saw you get popped."

"They made me clean up our mess," Jesse said. "I'm working there now."

"They looking for me?" Perry asked with a worried look.

Jesse shook his head and Perry grinned.

"That's cool," he said. "Hey, I'm sorry you got caught and had to work."

"No sweat," Jesse said. "So where you been staying?"

"That guy Dayton set me up," Perry said proudly. "I'm working for him now. I keep watch for cops and stuff. It's a good deal. Hey, I mentioned you to him. He said it was cool if you want to give it a try."

There had been a time when Jesse would have jumped at the chance to work for a heavy dude like Dayton. But that was before Willy.

"I don't know," Jesse said, looking at the damp bundle of newspaper in the bike's basket. "I better think about it."

"Snooze you lose," Perry said.

"Sure," Jesse said. "Hey, drop by the park sometime."

They gave each other high fives and then Jesse pedaled away, feeling funny.

* * *

A little while later, he arrived at the park and carried the bundle of newspaper into the amphitheater. Ever since the men had examined him, Willy had seemed restless and angry, constantly swimming in circles around the tank. Jesse hoped the fresh fish might help him feel better. He walked out onto the platform and unrolled the newspaper, revealing the scraps of fish. Then he picked up a piece and threw it into the water.

Willy stopped circling and approached it. But instead of eating the scrap, he simply took it in his mouth and swam toward Jesse.

"Hey, I thought you liked this stuff," Jesse said, but Willy just stared back at him. Jesse took the chunk of fish back and pretended to eat it. "See, you're supposed to eat it like this."

But Willy shook his head and swam away to the other side of the tank. Jesse sat down on the platform and stared at the water. He didn't understand why Willy wouldn't eat. Suddenly he had an idea and picked up a fistful of fish and held it out over the water.

"How about I put this in your mouth?" he asked Willy.

Willy swam slowly toward him. The next thing Jesse knew, the orca opened his mouth and swallowed the fish. Jesse grinned and quickly fed him the rest of the scraps. Then he rinsed off his hands in the tank water.

"I'll see you later, Willy," he said. "I have work

to do now." He rose and took a step back, but then stopped.

In the water, Willy swam backward and stopped, too, as if he was imitating Jesse. But was he really? Jesse took a step to the right. Willy rolled to the right, shadowing the boy's movement. Jesse moved to his left and Willy followed. He hopped three steps to the right and Willy rolled three times. Jesse jumped up and down and Willy spyhopped. Jesse jumped and spun around. Willy spyhopped and spun in the water. Jesse stood on his head. Willy turned upside down and stuck his tail out of the water.

Across the tank, unnoticed by both Willy and Jesse, Randolph and Rae stood and stared in amazement.

"Well," Randolph said in a low voice, "I think Willy has finally found himself a soul mate."

Rae couldn't believe it. Carrying a fish bucket, she stepped slowly and carefully toward the platform, as if worried she might break the magic spell. Jesse noticed her out of the corner of his eye, but kept right on playing with Willy.

"You can feed him?" Rae asked in wonder as she stepped out onto the platform.

Jesse reached into the bucket and picked up a chunk of fish and held it over the water. Willy came up and took it.

"You want to try it?" Jesse asked Rae.

Rae was dying to. She kneeled at the edge of

the platform and held out a piece of fish to Willy, but instead of taking it, the whale backed away. Rae sighed as if she understood.

"I don't get it," Jesse said.

"Come with me while I feed the sea lions and I'll explain," Rae said.

A few moments later they stood in front of the sea lion tank, throwing chunks of fish to the hungry animals.

"Willy and I didn't get off to a good start," Rae said. "He thinks I'm the wicked witch because of all the medical tests we had to do when we first got him. And he's still mad that we took him away from his family."

"Family?" Jesse asked, puzzled.

"Sure," Rae said. "Out in the ocean, killer whales live in families. Some of them spend their whole lives with their moms and never leave."

"Never?" Jesse was surprised. After all, they were just animals.

"Their social structure is very important to them," Rae explained. "Up to fifty orcas have been seen traveling together. Some will stay together their whole lives."

So maybe that's it, Jesse thought. Maybe he and Willy did have something in common. They'd both lost their families.

Rae finished feeding the sea lions and headed toward the trainer's room.

"Have you ever seen orcas out in the ocean?" Jesse asked as they walked.

Rae nodded. "My dad was in the Navy. He did sonar research on whales. I used to go out on the water with him all the time."

In the trainer's room were a couple of desks and a row of dented green lockers. Taped to the lockers were snapshots of the trainers with their favorite seals, sea lions, and porpoises. Jesse noticed some graphs on Rae's desk.

"Do you do research?" he asked.

"Not right now," Rae said. "I'm just a trainer here. But I want to work out on the ocean. I'm going back to school someday to get my Ph.D. in marine biology."

"But if you leave, Willy will be all alone," Jesse said.

"I know," Rae said, "but Charlie's in school. . . ."

"Who's Charlie?" Jesse asked.

Rae opened her locker. Taped to the inside was a black-and-white photo of a guy. "He's my boyfriend."

Jesse wasn't thrilled to hear that Rae had a boyfriend.

"Do you have a girlfriend?" Rae asked.

Jesse shrugged. "What makes you think I'd want one?"

"Just a guess," Rae said with a smile. While she turned to take her wet suit out of the locker,

64

Jesse looked at some charts on the wall. One was a chart of whales, and an orca was circled in red and marked Willy. But Jesse was puzzled.

"This isn't Willy," he said.

"Sure it is," Rae replied.

"But Willy's top fin is flopped over and this one's straight," he said, pointing at the picture.

"That seems to happen to killer whales when they're in captivity," Rae said. "No one knows why. Maybe they just need more room to swim."

"How come the owner of this place won't build a bigger tank?" Jesse asked.

"You're talking about Dial?" Rae said. She shrugged her shoulders. "He thinks Willy is just a commodity."

"A what?" Jesse said.

"It's a word Dial likes to use," Rae explained. "Basically, Dial won't build Willy a bigger tank unless he thinks it will make him more money." She paused for a second and thought. Suddenly she had a great idea. "Hey! Maybe you could help convince Dial to build Willy a bigger tank. What do you think?"

"Sure," Jesse said. "But how?"

Flushed with excitement, Rae sat down and told him her plan.

Later that evening when it was time to go, Jesse went to say good-bye to Willy. The setting sun had painted the clouds warm hues of pink and orange, and as Jesse entered the amphitheater, he could hear Willy's high-pitched squeal. He found the whale spyhopping, facing the edge of the tank overlooking the harbor.

"Hey, Willy," Jesse called, slapping the water with his hand to get the whale's attention. But Willy just ignored him and continued calling toward the ocean. Jesse didn't understand why Willy wouldn't come, but he decided to leave him alone and go home.

He was just passing Randolph's cabin when the Indian caretaker came out and waved to him.

"Hey, Jesse," he called. "I've got something for you."

Jesse climbed the stairs and went into the cabin. Inside, Randolph handed him an old brown leather-bound book with strange-looking writing on the cover.

"Uh, thanks," Jesse said, wondering why Randolph had given it to him.

"It's from the Haida," Randolph said. "That's my tribe."

Jesse was surprised. He knew Randolph was an Indian, but it had never occurred to him that he might come from a tribe. "Is your tribe still around?"

Randolph shook his head. "Not many of us now. But three hundred years ago we were a strong tribe. Back when there were so many fish in the water that our tribesmen only had to spend one day a week gathering food. And everyone ate like kings."

"What did they do the rest of the time?" Jesse asked.

"They painted, made music, told stories." Randolph reached over and took the book. He turned a few pages to an etching of a whale. "Here, I want to show you a story." He began to read. " 'Natsalane was a Haida Indian who lived many years ago before there were any orca whales. One day while fishing in a canoe with the other warriors, young Natsalane lost his way and found himself all alone.' "

Jesse listened with great interest.

" 'As Natsalane searched for the other warriors,' " Randolph read, " 'a fierce storm began. Natsalane couldn't find shelter, but the sea otters appeared and took him down under the sea where he was safe for the night. After the storm, Natsalane began searching again for the other braves, but all he found was a huge log. He carved a great beast out of the log and tried to carry it to the ocean, but it was too heavy. Finally he reached a pool of water and set the log beast down, but the carving dropped to the bottom of the pool and disappeared. So he said a prayer he had never heard before. *Salanaa Eiyung Ayesis.*' "

Randolph turned the book around and showed

Jesse an etching of Natsalane, the Indian brave, kneeling in anguish by the side of the pool where the carving had disappeared. Jesse watched, fascinated. . . . *Salanaa Eiyung Ayesis*.

That night in his room, Jesse paced the floor as he excitedly told the rest of the story to Annie, who sat on the bed and listened.

"So Natsalane's just waiting there," Jesse said. "And he keeps saying this prayer. *'Salanaa Eiyung Ayesis.'* And it's so weird because he never heard it before, but somehow he just knows it. But then all this water starts flying up from the pool and the next thing he knows, the carving comes floating up out of the water. Only now it's like a whale . . . like Willy! And it can fly like a bird. So Natsalane runs after it and he rides the whale all the way home." He paused and stared at Annie. "I mean, isn't that cool?"

"Yes, Jesse," Annie said with a warm smile. "It is."

For a moment Jesse and Annie just stared at each other. Inside, Jesse had this warm feeling. It was a feeling he hadn't had in a long time, not since his mother had gone away. Now he had it with Annie, except she wasn't his mother. Jesse turned away, feeling confused. Annie watched him and knew it was time to leave.

"Good night, Jesse," she said softly.

"Night," Jesse said. After she left, he lay down

on the bed and shut his eyes. He was very tired. It had been an incredible day. Rae had come up with a plan to help Willy, and Randolph had told him that amazing story. In no time, Jesse was asleep.

9

The next morning, Rae and Jesse went to work on their plan to help Willy. They stood on the trainer's platform next to the tank with a bucket of fish.

"Most orcas love to play around and do tricks," Rae said. "They love the stimulation."

As she spoke, Jesse peered down into the tank, searching for Willy. "Can he see me?"

Rae nodded. "He can hear you, too. From anywhere in the tank." She handed Jesse a long pole with a bright red pool float on its end. "This is a target. Willy is supposed to respond to it and learn to follow it. When we work on a trick or a behavior, you reward him with some fish."

Willy's long black back surfaced in the middle of the tank. Jesse could see one of the whale's large blue eyes through the water. He lifted the target and Willy turned his head slightly. Rae blew her whistle.

"Good," she said. "Toss him a fish."

Jesse was surprised. "But all he did was turn his head a little."

"That's plenty . . . for him," Rae said. "Go on, give him a fish."

Jesse threw Willy a piece of fish and then pulled the target across to his opposite side. Again, Willy reacted slightly. Rae blew her whistle and Jesse tossed another piece of fish.

"He's been exposed to all this a thousand times," Rae said. "Willy knows our signals. He knows what he's supposed to do. He just doesn't want to do anything for anybody."

Jesse moved the target and once again Willy responded. When Jesse threw him a piece of fish, Willy rolled in the water as if he enjoyed playing with Jesse. Rae laughed excitedly. Jesse noticed that Randolph had stopped nearby to watch.

"Most orcas love to be touched, patted, hugged, anything like that," Rae said. "They love to have their tongues stroked."

Jesse stared at her in disbelief. "You want me to put my hand in Willy's mouth?"

"Maybe eventually," Rae said with a smile. "You'll get to know him. Then you should be able to do that."

For the next two weeks, Jesse and Rae worked with Willy. The whale began to respond more and more, and Rae couldn't help noticing that both Willy *and* his new young trainer seemed to grow happier every day. The Greenwoods noticed it, too. At home, Jesse seemed friendlier and his appetite was growing.

By the end of two weeks, Jesse and Willy seemed like best friends. Jesse had made a toy of plastic pop bottles tied together with string and Willy loved playing with it. One afternoon, Jesse threw the toy out into the tank and Willy brought it right back to the platform. Jesse kneeled down and took the toy from Willy's lips. Instead of swimming away, the big whale floated near the platform with his mouth open in a smile.

Jesse glanced at Rae, who nodded. Then he slowly reached out and stroked Willy's huge pink tongue. Willy opened his mouth wider and rolled his eyes.

"He loves it!" Rae whispered.

At home that night, Annie asked Jesse to take some dinner down to the auto repair shop since Glen was working late. Jesse took the plate wrapped in foil and put it in the basket of his bike and rode down to the shop. He'd never actually been there before. He'd always pictured auto shops as dirty, greasy places, but Glen's was very clean and orderly. Even at that late hour, several mechanics in dark green coveralls were working on cars. One of them was cutting sheet metal with an electric arc torch that threw off a blue light so bright Jesse had to shield his eyes.

Jesse found Glen in his office with a pile of paperwork on the desk in front of him and a phone against his ear. When he saw Jesse come in, he covered the phone with his hand.

"Jesse," he said with a smile. "What's up?"

"Annie sent me with dinner," Jesse said, putting the covered plate down on the desk.

"Great. Thanks," Glen said. He looked down at the phone in his hands and frowned. "Darn, I forgot who I was holding for." But he put the phone back against his ear anyway.

Jesse looked around the office, surprised to see a small snapshot of himself tucked into the frame of a larger photo of Annie. Near it was a gold trophy from an automobile show and a framed photo of a sleek-looking red car with a white hood and round windows in the sides.

"So you got it in stock?" Glen said into the phone. "Okay, Brody, I'll send a guy over in the morning."

He hung up and noticed that Jesse was looking at the trophy and the photo of the car.

"Fifty-eight T-bird," Glen said.

"Neat car," said Jesse.

"A classic," Glen said proudly.

Then Jesse picked up a photo of Glen and Annie. "You and Annie ever fight?" Jesse asked.

"Yeah. We schedule one every couple of months. Why?"

"Just asking." Jesse could see that Glen was

kidding him. The only reason he asked was because his mother always used to fight with her boyfriends. Jesse turned and spotted another photo. This was an old black-and-white one of a smiling boy and an older woman.

"Is that you?" Jesse asked.

Glen nodded. "Check out that smile. Used to be all I needed."

"Who's the lady?" Jesse asked.

"My mom."

"Where is she now?"

"She died a couple of years ago," Glen said.

"My mom's gonna be coming to get me one of these days," Jesse said.

"She is?" Glen looked confused.

Jesse nodded. "It won't be too long now."

"But I thought they told me . . ." Glen let the words trail off. Jesse glared at him, his hands becoming fists.

"You don't believe me?" Jesse asked.

"Well, I, uh, was under the impression that . . ." Again Glen let his words trail off, but Jesse knew what he was going to say and it made him angry.

"I don't care what they said!" he yelled. "They don't know nothing!"

"Okay, okay." Glen lifted his hands and Jesse calmed down a little.

"My mom's just got some things to take care

of," he said. "When she's done, she's coming for me."

Glen just nodded. Jesse could see his foster father didn't believe him. All of a sudden Jesse didn't want to stay there and talk to Glen anymore. He went out to his bike and rode away.

It was getting late and it had started to rain. In the smoky video arcade, Jesse stood lost in thought. All around him kids were glued to the glowing, flashing games, blasting and smashing and killing everything on the screens. The air was filled with cigarette smoke and explosions, screeches and the *rat-tat-tat* of rapid-fire guns. Jesse felt strangely comforted, as if what was going on around him matched what he was feeling inside. And yet somehow, it didn't feel quite right.

As much as he hated to admit it, this video arcade wasn't where he wanted to be. He went outside, got on his bike, and left.

Several miles away, Annie sat at the kitchen table in her house, nervously twisting a paper napkin into little pieces. The kitchen door swung open and she quickly looked up, hoping to see Jesse, but it was only Glen.

"He hasn't been to the park," Glen said as he stepped inside and put his car keys on the key hook by the kitchen door.

"You think we should call Dwight?" Annie asked.

Glen shrugged and slipped out of his wet raincoat.

"It's after eleven," Annie said anxiously.

"I know what time it is," Glen snapped irritably at her. He saw the surprise in his wife's eyes and quickly apologized. "Sorry, Annie, I'm just worried, too."

A moment later the door opened behind them and Jesse stepped in, his brown hair and jacket soaked with rain.

"Jesse!" Annie jumped up from her chair. "Where were you? We were going crazy with worry."

Jesse just stared at the floor.

"I thought we agreed that you'd let us know where you were," Glen said angrily.

Jesse shrugged. "Doesn't matter."

"What do you mean, it doesn't matter?" Glen asked.

Jesse glared at him. "You want to dump on me? Go ahead. I don't care. I live here the same way I lived on the streets. Always ready to move on. Understand?"

Glen and Annie were taken aback by the anger in his voice. They watched silently as he left the kitchen. A moment later they heard a door slam upstairs. Annie slumped into the kitchen chair.

"I . . . I thought we were making progress with

him," she said with a sad, slow shake of her head.

"I know," Glen said, leaning against the kitchen counter. "Just when you think you're getting through, making some kind of connection . . . then *whammo* suddenly you're in a free-fall."

"I think he's scared, Glen," Annie said. "That's why he's pushing us away."

"I'd like to give him a push all right," Glen muttered. "Right out the door."

Up in his room, Jesse sat on his bed, feeling a million angry emotions surging through him. He could hear Annie and Glen talking downstairs. He couldn't make out the words, but his foster parents sounded upset. On the shelf across the room, he spotted that little box Annie had given him when he'd first arrived. He got up and tore the box open. Inside was a baseball and a little note that said: *Welcome to our family.*

Downstairs, the discussion was growing louder and angrier. Jesse quietly walked to his door and opened it enough to hear.

"You know the real reason you're angry, don't you?" Annie was asking.

"No," Glen replied angrily. "What's the *real* reason?"

"You've got feelings for him and it scares you," Annie said. "You don't like that."

"You're right, I don't," Glen said. "Look Annie, we don't owe anybody anything. We tried with the kid. We did our part. That's all we had to do."

Jesse's eyes went wide. The argument sounded like so many he'd heard when he was young. It frightened and upset him. Were they really going to get rid of him? Throw him out?

"Don't turn this into one of your crusades, Annie," Glen was saying.

"Okay, okay." It sounded like Annie was crying. "Maybe I do turn things into crusades. Maybe that's the way I am."

"Annie, I'm happy" — Glen's voice grew softer — "with just you and me."

"That's fine for you," Annie sniffed, "but I'm not happy."

"Okay, if you want a child that badly, let's go ahead and adopt a newborn," Glen said.

Jesse felt as if the wind had been knocked out of him. So they were going to get rid of him and adopt a baby! Furious, he spun around and hurled the baseball through the window.

In his anger, Jesse didn't hear Annie tell Glen that she wouldn't let Jesse go. The boy needed them.

Downstairs, Glen heard the window shatter. "What the . . . ?" He rushed out of the kitchen and up the stairs.

Glen and Annie hurried into Jesse's room. They found Jesse with his face pressed into the pillow and his fists clenched.

"Jesse," Annie said, sliding her hands around his shoulders. "Are you okay?"

Meanwhile, Glen silently surveyed the broken window.

"I just got scared," Jesse said, still hiding his face in the pillow.

"Scared of what?" Annie asked.

Jesse turned and looked at her. "I heard you guys fighting."

Annie and Glen looked shocked. Glen kneeled next to the bed and spoke softly. "I'd never hurt Annie, never. And I'd never hurt you. You ought to know that."

"Yeah, okay." Jesse nodded. His foster father sounded like he really meant it.

Glen sighed and glanced again at the broken window. "Guess you got our housewarming present."

"Yeah, thanks," Jesse said with an embarrassed grin.

10

The big day was nearing and Jesse was still busy working with Willy. Jesse had grown to like the whale so much that he spent all the money he made, at the fish market buying Willy salmon instead of the junk Dial and Wade wanted him to eat.

One hot, sunny afternoon, while Jesse fed Willy a whole salmon, a finger tapped him on the shoulder. Jesse turned to find Perry behind him. Only, it was a different Perry than before. His friend was wearing a gold chain around his neck and his clothes looked new. Instead of old sneakers, he was wearing a shiny pair of black boots. He would have looked pretty neat were it not for a black eye and his pasty white skin.

"Hey, dude!" Perry grinned and slapped Jesse five. As Jesse watched, his friend tapped a cigarette out of a pack and lit it with a silver lighter.

In the tank, Willy rose to the surface and eyed him.

"Whoa," Perry gasped. "What's that?"

"It's an orca," Jesse said. "Killer whale."

"Awesome." Perry grinned, then coughed as he exhaled smoke. "So I just wanted to tell you I'm leaving town, dude. First to Sacramento, then L.A. Dayton and I are like business partners now."

"Sounds pretty cool," Jesse said, a little enviously. It was obvious that Perry was making good money. He felt a little funny. It seemed as if Perry's plan had really worked. Jesse had never expected his friend to actually start living the dream.

"So look," Perry said. "I just wanted to tell you there's still time for you to get in on it with me and Dayton."

For a split second Jesse was tempted. Then he glanced back at Willy. "Thanks, but I can't right now."

Perry couldn't hide his disappointment. "Okay, fool, be that way." He reached into his pocket and handed Jesse a postcard that said, VENICE BEACH in bright red letters and showed two pretty blonde women in skimpy bikinis roller blading. "This is where we're going. If you ever get the guts to go, look me up."

The next thing Jesse knew, Perry turned

around and walked out of the amphitheater. Jesse sat down on the edge of the tank and stared into the water. Wow, it really looked like Perry had finally hit the big time.

Nearby, Willy surfaced and swam slowly toward him. Jesse sighed, then reached over and patted the whale on the head. "You miss your family, Willy?"

It actually seemed as if Willy nodded.

"My mom's a pain," Jesse said. "She couldn't take care of me. She couldn't even take care of herself. I haven't seen her since I was a little kid. But I . . . I still miss her. The Greenwoods are okay, I guess. It's rough. I'm nervous around them, but that's just the way it is. Could be a lot worse. Really."

In the water, Willy chirped and let out a low squeal. Jesse took out his harmonica and tried to imitate the sounds the whale made. To his surprise, Willy seemed to sing back. Then the whale came close and nudged him with his great black nose. Jesse put down his harmonica and reached forward, sliding his hand over Willy's sleek back to his dorsal fin. The next thing he knew, Willy started to back away, slowly pulling Jesse into the water with him.

Go in the tank? Jesse hesitated, but it was awfully hot and sunny . . . and a swim would be fun. Especially a swim with Willy. Still holding the whale's dorsal fin, Jesse slid into the chilly green water. Willy started to swim and then dove. Jesse held on tight, flying through the water beside the whale. It was incredible! He felt like he was going so fast! As if he were almost a fish himself! And just when Jesse felt like he was going to run out of breath, Willy rose to the surface to let him get some fresh air.

Jesse climbed onto Willy's back and rode the whale like a horse. Again they took off around the tank, with Jesse laughing loudly. He couldn't ever remember having so much fun.

Finally, the big day arrived. Rae had invited Dial and Wade to see the progress Jesse had made with Willy. She told Jesse that if the owner and manager liked what they saw, they might agree to give Willy a big show. And if the show made money, they'd be able to build Willy a bigger tank. The men sat in the empty amphitheater while Rae stood with Jesse on the trainer's platform.

"Okay, kid," Rae said, putting her hand on Jesse's shoulder. "Time to show 'em your stuff."

Jesse leaned over the edge of the tank, where Willy floated, watching him. "Want to do some tricks?" he asked.

Willy nodded yes. Jesse gave him a signal and Willy responded by squirting Jesse in the face with water. It was all part of the show, but Jesse pretended it wasn't.

"Hey, Willy," he said, wiping the water off his

face and pretending to be annoyed. "Don't squirt me. Go squirt everyone else."

Under Jesse's direction, Willy swam around the pool on his back slapping the water with his tail. Then he stood on his head with his tail sticking ten feet up in the air.

"Hey, Willy!" Jesse shouted. "Want to play ball?"

He threw a large red ball to Willy, who caught it in his mouth and blew it back, shaking his head.

Jesse caught the ball. "Okay, you don't want to play ball. How about some barrel rolls?"

Willy responded by rolling and rolling in the water, around the tank. Out of the corner of his eye, Jesse could see the manager and owner of the park nodding with approval, but the best was yet to come. Jesse gave Willy a signal and the whale took off, circling the tank as fast as he could swim. Then suddenly he veered toward the trainer's platform and slid up onto it, completely out of the water. Willy lifted his tail and opened his mouth in a smile. Jesse beamed and patted his friend on the side of the head.

Smiling proudly, Rae turned to Dial and Wade. "And that, gentlemen, is our show."

The owner and manager seemed pleased. They waved for Rae and Jesse to join them in the amphitheater seats. Jesse gave Rae a nervous look, but Rae nodded back at him, indicating that for Willy's sake, they had to go. As they climbed the steps, Jesse could feel their eyes on him.

"Well, that was pretty good," said Dial. "But here's my question. How do you know you can do it again?"

Jesse glanced at Rae, who nodded. "If you'll just give us a chance, I know Willy will come through."

Dial rubbed his smoothly shaved jaw. "What you want will cost a lot of money. I have to be sure." He turned to Jesse. "What does the kid say?"

Jesse nodded his head. "Yes, sir. I assure you Willy and I can do it again anytime."

Dial sat back and stared up at the sky as he thought. "Okay," he finally said. "Set it up."

Jesse could hardly contain his excitement. He and Willy were going to do a big show! He dashed off to the sea lion's tank, where Randolph was cementing a crack.

"It's happening!" he gasped. "They're into it."

"I told you it could happen!" The caretaker grinned and patted Jesse on the back. "Dial's pretty thick, but he had to see the light on this one."

Meanwhile, back in the amphitheater, Dial and Wade stood alone, watching Willy swim by himself in the main tank.

"This could be worthwhile," Dial mused. "Maybe we can turn this thing around after all."

Next to him, Wade nodded slowly. "It's going

to cost us plenty to set up the show."

"So what?" Dial asked. "We let the kid work up a presentation. If it catches on, we're on our way. Just like we planned."

On the morning of the show, Glen and Annie sat at the kitchen table, almost too excited to eat.

"Look at this," Glen said, pointing to a full-page ad in the local newspaper for Willy's show.

"And they were advertising it on the radio this morning," Annie said. "I bet they get a huge crowd."

The kitchen door swung open and Jesse stepped in, wearing his new blue-and-green whale trainer's wet suit. Like Rae's it had an emblem of an orca on the front.

"Wow!" Annie clapped her hands together.

"Hey, is that a spot already?" Glen asked, pointing at the emblem on Jesse's chest. Jesse looked down and Glen quickly flipped his finger against Jesse's nose. "Gotcha!"

They all laughed.

"You guys ready?" Jesse asked nervously.

"Don't you want some breakfast?" Annie asked.

"I'm not hungry," Jesse said. The truth was, his stomach was knotted with nervousness.

"Okay, everyone," Glen said, getting up. "Let's get this show on the road."

The Northwest Adventure Park hadn't looked so good since the day it opened. Signs and walls were freshly painted. Banners and balloons flew everywhere. Clowns dressed like killer whales entertained crowds of kids. In the underwater observation room beside the main tank, children peered through the windows into the water for a glimpse of Willy and banged their fists on the glass to get his attention.

In the trainer's room, Jesse sat at a mirror, pulling a comb through his hair and listening to the crowd noises as people shouted and moved into the amphitheater. Rae came up behind him.

"There are a lot of people out there," she said. "You nervous?"

"No," Jesse lied.

Rae slid a small paper bag onto the table in front of him. "Here's a little present from Randolph and me."

Jesse looked surprised as he opened the bag and took out a shiny whale whistle on a leather strap.

"Cool," Jesse said, sliding the whistle over his head. "Thanks."

"Break a leg, kid." Rae winked and started out. As she pulled open the door, Jesse recognized Dwight standing out in the hall.

"Hey, Dwight." Jesse gave him a shy smile. "I didn't think you'd come."

"You serious?" Dwight gave him a big smile. "This is too exciting to miss. I'm really proud of you, man."

Jesse knew Dwight really meant it. "Thanks," he said.

"Hey, Jesse!" someone shouted from outside. "It's time!"

As Jesse trotted down the corridor under the amphitheater, he could hear Rae on the loudspeaker outside: "Ladies and gentlemen, presenting the superstar orca of Northwest Adventure Park. Let's hear it for Willy!"

As the crowd clapped, Jesse came out on the trainer's platform carrying a bucket of fish. The crowd in the amphitheater around him seemed huge. Across the tank, Willy surfaced with a great burst of spray and swam toward him.

"Willy's young friend is Jesse," Rae told the crowd over the loudspeaker. "Today Jesse and Willy have a special show for you."

Seated high up in the amphitheater, Dial and Wade could feel the eager anticipation of the crowd around them, but Wade was worried.

"That kid looks tiny out there," he said. "It looks like we get our trainers out of kindergarten."

"It's all part of the charm," Dial said with a smile. "I'm telling you, Wade, this could be big. Really big."

On the platform, Jesse reached down and patted Willy on the head. "Okay, big guy, let's show 'em your stuff." He gave Willy a hand signal and the killer whale obediently dove from the surface.

Beside the tank, in the underwater observation

room, the crowds of children kept banging their fists against the glass. Willy had heard that banging sound before . . . the day he was captured.

Up on the platform, Jesse raised a fist into the air. It was a signal that Willy was supposed to jump.

But Willy didn't jump.

Jesse felt his stomach grow tight as he repeated the signal. *Come on, Willy!* he thought quietly.

The crowd in the amphitheater grew quiet. Jesse glanced nervously at Rae, who quickly got back on the loudspeaker. "Willy is a twelve-year-old adolescent orca. He's twenty-two feet long and weighs three and a half tons."

To Jesse's surprise, Willy surfaced next to the platform, looking sad and scared. But Jesse didn't see it. He was too worried about making the show a success.

"Come on, Willy," he whispered. "You know the signals."

But Willy just stared up at him. The banging of the children's fists against the glass was still ringing in his ears. Just like the banging sound the men had made on the boats when Willy was first captured. Up in the stands, Wade and Dial gave each other a look.

"What's going on?" Dial asked.

Wade answered with a shrug.

Jesse quickly gave Willy some fish and then made a circle with his outstretched arm, a signal for Willy to dance on his tail. But Willy, growing more and more distracted by the terrible banging noises coming from the observation window, just sank beneath the surface.

In the audience, someone booed. Jesse's head snapped up. He felt scared and angry, standing alone before the big crowd. Again, Rae got on the loudspeaker.

"Like every performer," she told the crowd, "Willy gets stage fright once in a while."

But the boos grew louder.

"Ladies and gentlemen, please," Rae pleaded.

Jesse felt everyone staring at him. Willy still wouldn't come up. Jesse couldn't stand the boos and jeers any longer. He turned and ran from the platform.

In the tank below, the growing sound of hands banging against the glass terrified Willy. Finally, he turned and swam straight at the children.

Crash! Willy hit the glass so hard, a few bolts popped from the window's frame and created a small leak. Terrified children screamed and started running out of the underwater observation room.

Up in the stands, Wade also heard the crash. He jumped out of his seat and ran down toward the observation room. As he tried to get down the stairs, he had to fight his way through a crowd of screaming kids. Finally Wade made it inside. He could see the broken bolts in the window frame and the small rivulet of leaking water. It had never occurred to him that the whale could hit the glass so hard he'd create a leak. As he stared at the window, a thought began to form in his head . . .

The last thing Rae told the crowd was that the adventure park would be glad to refund their tickets. Then she went down to the trainer's room, where she found Jesse peeling off his new wet suit.

"I guess Willy wasn't ready to perform," Rae said.

"I guess not," Jesse said angrily.

"It's not your fault, Jesse," Rae said softly.

It didn't matter whose fault it was. The whole thing was just stupid. Jesse wished he'd never gotten involved with that dumb whale in the first place. He ran out the back door of the amphitheater, so angry he kicked the first trash can he saw.

Ow! It hurt his foot. Now even angrier, Jesse kicked it again. This time he knocked it over and all the garbage spilled out. He was just about to turn to the next trash can when he heard a voice behind him.

"Wait, Jesse. I'll hold it. You kick it."

Jesse spun around. Dwight, Annie, and Glen were standing behind him.

"It takes a lot a courage to work with an animal

that big and strong," Annie said softly.

"Maybe Willy just doesn't want to be a performer," Glen added.

Jesse just stared angrily at the ground.

"Hey, look," Glen said, stepping closer. "You gave it your best shot. You worked hard. You did everything you could. Jesse, you did great."

"We're proud of you," Annie said.

Jesse just shook his head. Annie could see he wasn't really listening, but she kept trying to reach him anyway. "I'd get nervous, too, if I had to do tricks in front of all those people."

Jesse didn't need these stupid foster parents and their phony attempts to make him feel better. He turned and started to walk away. Annie started after him, but Dwight waved at her to stop. Then Dwight himself jogged after Jesse.

"Hey, what's up?" the burly social worker asked. "The show isn't — "

"Forget the show!" Jesse shouted.

"But the Greenwoods," Dwight began.

"Forget the Greenwoods!"

Dwight stopped. "Now they're against you, too?"

Jesse nodded. "Just like everything else."

"I don't think you have such a bad thing with them," Dwight said.

"Then you live there!" Jesse shouted. "I'm sick of this place. I'm going to find my mom."

"Your mom?" Dwight asked, shocked.

"You heard me," Jesse said as he started to run again. "I'm going to find my mom."

Dwight jogged ahead and blocked Jesse's path. "Listen. The federal government can't find your mom. The state can't find her."

"Well, I'll find her!" Jesse shouted. He tried to step around Dwight, but the big man grabbed Jesse's shoulders and kneeled in front of him. Suddenly they were face-to-face.

"When are you going to get it, Jesse?" he asked angrily. "Your mom isn't coming back. You forget the day she dropped you on our doorstep? Well, I remember. She turned around and drove away, Jesse. She didn't slow down, didn't turn around, didn't even look in the rearview mirror. Does that sound like somebody's momma to you?"

Jesse looked away. Dwight caught his breath and continued. "Now you got two people over here who want to be your friends. That's more than your mother *ever* was. You could use a friend right now, Jesse, because if you keep dreaming about finding your mother you're going to end up losing big time. You got that?"

Jesse could feel the tears surge out of his eyes. He quickly squirmed out of the big man's grip. "Get out of here!" he shouted. "What are you doing? I don't need this now!"

Before Dwight could stop him, Jesse ran.

11

The sun was setting over the ocean. Jesse stood at the edge of the roadway in the middle of the bridge, staring out at the pink and orange clouds and the orange sunlight rippling on the surface of the harbor. He knew Glen and Annie were parked in the tow truck in the middle of the bridge behind him, waiting. But he didn't care. Let 'em wait. He'd waited for his mother, but she never came. He'd waited for Willy and that had been a total waste.

He figured the Greenwoods would probably get tired of waiting and drive away.

But they stayed.

And finally, after the sun went down, he walked back to the truck and got in.

Later, Jesse lay in bed, the blankets pulled up over his shoulder, staring glumly at the window he'd broken. Glen had covered it with plastic. The door to his room opened slowly and Annie came in.

"I feel bad for Willy," she said.

"Me, too," said Jesse.

"You know, animals can sometimes misbehave," she said. "Just like people. That doesn't mean you should lose faith in them, right?"

Jesse didn't answer. Everybody he'd ever cared about had misbehaved. They'd all let him down. He just wanted Annie to leave. Finally she said good night and closed the door. Jesse waited until he heard her footsteps go back down the stairs, then he quietly slid out of bed. He was still wearing his clothes.

He sat up and took the postcard Perry had given him out of his pocket, and stared at the girls in bikinis, roller blading. He slid the card back into his pocket, picked up his backpack, and quietly slid the window open. This time he was going to misbehave first. He was going to get out of there before the Greenwoods had a chance to disappoint him, too.

A little while later, Jesse snuck into the adventure park and walked quietly into the amphitheater. He sat down at the edge of the main tank, his emotions still a confused whirl. Near him, Willy surfaced and pushed the toy Jesse had made of plastic pop bottles toward him.

Jesse angrily picked up the toy and threw it back into the tank, but Willy quickly retrieved it.

"Sure," Jesse said bitterly. "Now you want to do tricks. So what happened before? You choked, didn't you?"

Willy squirted a little water toward Jesse.

"Cut it out," Jesse snapped irritably. "Just forget about it." He reached into his pocket and pulled out the whale whistle Rae and Randolph had given him. With a mighty heave, he threw it into the tank and turned away.

Behind him, Willy let out a low sad whistle. Jesse stopped and turned. "Don't start that now. I'm out of here. I'm going to California, okay? Have a good life, Willy."

Behind him, Willy's lament grew louder. Jesse felt so bad that tears started to fall from his eyes. But this time he'd had enough, he really had. He was leaving for good.

Willy cried even louder. Jesse couldn't help turning back one last time. To his surprise, he saw that Willy wasn't even looking at him. He was facing the edge of the tank that looked out toward the harbor, spy hopping as high as he could as if he were trying to see something.

Now Jesse heard something else. It sounded like Willy's sad call, only much fainter, like it was coming from out in the harbor somewhere. Willy called again and again and the distant sound seemed to be answering. Puzzled, Jesse climbed up to the edge of the amphitheater to see.

And there in the moonlight was the most amazing sight — five spy hopping whales out in the harbor, calling back to Willy.

His family! Jesse realized. Rae had said they sometimes stayed together for life.

For several minutes the calls went back and forth. Jesse could hear the pain in Willy's squeals as he yearned to be back with his family. Jesse realized he'd heard that call many times before.

Just like me, Jesse thought. Except Willy knew where his family was.

As if sensing that what they wanted was impossible, the pod of whales out in the harbor slowly gave up and started to swim away. But Willy remained spy hopping in his tank, calling and calling in vain.

Jesse stared down at the tank, feeling so bad for him.

And then he saw something strange. It looked like a bright blue light flickering up through the tank from the underwater observation room.

Something told Jesse not to go down there. But he had to see what was going on. Quietly, he rushed down the stairs to the observation deck. As he got closer, he could make out the shadows of several men working, and the clanking sound of metal striking metal.

He couldn't believe what he saw. Wade was holding a flashlight while a man cut something with an arc torch like the one they used in Glen's auto repair shop. When he finished, a third man swung a hammer down hard and a bolt snapped off.

Suddenly Jesse realized what they were doing. Water was spraying out from around the bottom of the observation window. Willy wouldn't have much time before the tank was drained completely dry. Jesse turned and ran.

Seconds later he was pounding on the door to Randolph's cabin in the dark. "Randolph!" he shouted. "Wake up! Wake up!"

It seemed to take forever before the caretaker opened the door.

"There's a hole in Willy's tank!" Jesse cried.

Randolph quickly followed him back to the observation room. By now the pressure of the escaping water had pushed the window out and even more water was pouring out of the tank.

"They're trying to kill Willy!" Jesse shouted as he stood knee-deep in the roaring water.

"You're absolutely sure you saw Wade with them?" Randolph asked as he tried to see if the leak could be stopped.

"I swear," Jesse said.

"Wow." Randolph shook his head, dismayed. "Dial's trying to cash out on Willy."

"How?" Jesse asked.

"He's after the insurance money," Randolph said angrily. "Dial can't get Willy to work, and no one will buy him. So he's going to kill him and collect the insurance. A whale like Willy's probably worth a million dollars."

Through the windows, Jesse could see that the water level in the tank was still dropping. Willy swam by, looking frantic. Jesse realized that simply saving him wouldn't be enough. Dial might try some other way to kill him. Then he had an idea.

"Randolph!" he shouted. "We have to free Willy."

"What?" The caretaker looked at him as if he were crazy.

"Let's get him out of this place," Jesse said. "We could take him down to the harbor and put him back in the real water."

"You serious?" Randolph asked.

"Come on, man, why not?" Jesse asked.

Randolph scratched his head and shrugged. "I never liked this job that much anyway."

"Great!" Jesse grinned.

While Randolph went to get the whale harness, Jesse ran back to his cottage and called Rae. A little while later, while Randolph and Jesse were setting up the harness, they were suddenly bathed in headlights. Rae jumped out of her car.

"You're serious about this?" she asked, incredulously.

"Yes, and you're going to help us," Jesse said.

"Me?" Rae swallowed.

"That's right, lady," Randolph said.

Rae looked shocked. "But what about — "

"Look!" Randolph shouted. "All I know is this whale is going to die if he's dry-docked for too long. And this tank is way beyond repair."

"He's got a family out there," Jesse told her. "I saw them tonight. I heard them calling back and forth. Don't you get it? Willy's homesick. That's why he acts so weird."

Rae still didn't move. She seemed paralyzed with indecision.

"They tried to kill him!" Jesse shouted at her.

"Lift it, Jesse," Randolph said, and together they started to drag the slinglike harness toward the forklift.

"Did you call the police?" Rae asked.

"Aw, come on, Rae," Randolph said. "What can they do? If we don't get Willy into the water soon, he's going to die."

But Rae still couldn't move. She knew what they were doing was so wrong, and yet so right.

"Look, Rae," Randolph shouted, "either get out of here or turn on the number-two pump line, okay?"

It seemed as if he'd made Rae's mind up for

her. A moment later she ran to the pump and turned the handle as hard as she could.

They hooked the whale harness up to the forklift and drove it up to the holding tank. Out in the main tank, Willy was still swimming around frantically, aware that something was very wrong. Rae shoved a bucket of fish into Jesse's hand.

"You have to get him into the holding tank," she shouted.

Jesse quickly ran toward the main tank and shouted, "Willy, come on!"

But the frightened whale ignored him. Even the offer of handfuls of fish didn't help.

"Come on, Willy!" Jesse shouted at him. "We're trying to save your life. If you're so smart, how about giving us a little help, okay?"

A loud crash came from the underwater observation room.

"The window caved in!" Rae cried.

The level of water in the main tank started dropping faster. Jesse knew if he didn't do something fast, the water level would drop so low he'd never be able to get Willy into the holding tank. In a flash he vaulted over the wall and into the churning waters in the tank.

"Jesse!" Randolph shouted.

"Get out of there!" Rae screamed.

But Jesse ignored them and swam through the turbulent water to Willy.

"Willy!" he cried. "Come on! Now!"

Willy surfaced near him and studied him with one of his great blue eyes. Jesse stared right back.

"We're getting out of here," he said firmly. "Come on now, you have to help us."

Willy didn't move. Jesse felt tears of frustration well up in his eyes. "Willy, *please*," he begged. "This is your last chance."

And then, as if by a miracle, Willy swam into the holding tank.

It took a while to get the harness around him. Rae helped Jesse out of the tank while Randolph gunned the forklift's engine and gently raised Willy out of the water. With Rae and Jesse jogging behind, Randolph backed the forklift away from the holding tank and toward a 20-foot flatbed trailer covered with foam pads. Willy moaned softly as he was lowered onto the pads.

"How do you think he's doing?" Jesse asked Rae as he stroked the whale's nose.

"He's okay," Rae said. "Willy's been moved before. As long as we keep watering him down, he'll be fine."

Randolph unhitched the harness and jumped down from the forklift.

"Okay," he said. "We've got him on the trailer. Now how do we move it?"

* * *

It only took a few minutes for Randolph to drive Jesse over to the Greenwoods' house at that time of night. Jesse quietly opened the kitchen door and slipped Glen's car keys off the key hook. Then he snuck into the dark garage where Randolph was waiting.

"Ahh!" Randolph shouted with surprise.

"Shh!" Jesse pressed his finger to his lips.

"Didn't anyone ever tell you not to sneak up on people?" Randolph scolded him. Then he paused and looked around. "Where's Glen?"

"There's no time," Jesse said, tossing him the keys. "Besides, he wouldn't help."

They quietly opened the garage door and pushed the tow truck out, jumping into the cab as it rolled down the driveway. In the driver's seat, Randolph fumbled with the keys.

"Hurry up!" Jesse hissed.

"I'm hurrying," Randolph hissed back.

But he wasn't fast enough. Before he could get the truck started, it backed into a couple of garbage cans with a loud crash.

In the bedroom, Glen heard the crash and jumped out of bed. By the time he got to the window, Randolph had started the tow truck and it roared off into the night.

"Darn!" Glen swore.

"What, honey?" Annie asked from the bed.

"Someone just stole the truck!" Glen flicked on the lights and picked up the phone to call the police. Annie had a premonition and ran up to Jesse's room. By the time she got back, Glen had finished giving the police the description of the truck and its license number.

"Glen," Annie gasped. "Jesse's not here. His things are gone."

Glen and Annie stared at each other. "Let's get down to the shop," Glen said.

12

Back at the park, they hitched the tow truck up to the trailer with Willy on it.

"I say we go out to Dawson's Marina," Randolph shouted as they sprayed Willy down with water from portable sprayers.

"Sounds good," Rae shouted back. "It's the closest ocean access. We'd just better stick to the back roads."

In the commotion, they didn't hear the CB in the tow truck blare on as Glen called from the repair shop, asking Jesse if he was in the truck. Jesse himself was patting Willy on the head.

"It seems like he's breathing awful heavily," Jesse said, his words filled with concern.

"Don't worry, Jesse," Rae tried to reassure him. "Willy's going to make it."

"Okay, let's go!" Randolph shouted. Rae jumped in the cab with him. Jesse climbed up on the trailer to be with Willy. A second later, they pulled away from the amphitheater and headed for the bridge.

In the darkness of his bedroom, Dial held the phone to his ear in disbelief.

"You're crazy," he said. "Nobody would steal a whale."

"I'm telling you, that whale is gone!" Wade shouted on the other end. "The trailer's gone and the forklift's been moved around. That big-mouthed trainer and the Indian must have taken it."

"This is a disaster!" Dial gasped, sitting straight up in bed. "We don't have theft insurance on the whale! Call Wilson. Tell him to bring his crew down there."

In the repair shop, Glen turned off the CB. "It's no use. They're not answering in the truck."

"All right." Annie turned and marched out of the shop.

"Where are you going?" Glen asked.

"To look for him, of course," Annie said.

"That's ridiculous," Glen sputtered. "If he took the truck, the cops will find him."

"I don't want the cops to find him," Annie said flatly and got into the car. She reached for her keys and realized her husband had them. "Glen," she said, poking her head out the window, "give me those keys."

"There's no way I can convince you not to do this?" Glen asked.

"No." Annie shook her head.

"Okay." Glen sighed and pulled open the car door. "Move over. I'll drive."

Trying to avoid the main roads, they turned the truck down a narrow side road into a deserted, forested area. As they drove on, the road seemed to get narrower and narrower and the forest around them grew thicker. Suddenly Randolph jammed on the brakes. Riding on the trailer with Willy, Jesse jumped up to see what the matter was. He saw a huge tree trunk lying across the road illuminated by the truck's headlights.

"No way we can get around that," Randolph said in the truck's cab. "We'll have to back up."

It was hard to see going backward. They went a few yards in the dark and suddenly Jesse realized the trailer was starting to slip off the road and onto the muddy shoulder. The truck's wheels began to spin and whine in the mud. Randolph tried to put the truck into forward, but the trailer began to slide sideways and tip slightly.

"Randolph, *stop!*" Jesse shouted.

Randolph and Rae jumped out of the cab to see what was wrong.

"It's starting to tilt," Jesse gasped.

Randolph could see that he was right. "Maybe I could inch her forward."

But Rae shook her head. Her skin was almost white and she looked scared. "If that trailer tilts any farther, we may lose Willy."

A few miles away, Glen and Annie pulled into a brightly lit truck stop. The parking lot was filled with big semirigs, and Glen was hoping someone might have seen his tow truck on the road.

An old gray-haired fellow wearing greasy overalls stepped out of the truck stop cafe. Glen recognized him.

"Hey, Brody," he called. "You heard anything about a stolen tow truck?"

The old man looked up startled. "That your truck, Glen?"

"I'm afraid so," Glen admitted.

"The whale yours, too?" Brody asked with a big grin.

"Did you say whale?" Annie gasped.

"Sure," Brody said. "We heard Ed call in on the police band. They're all out there looking for a tow truck, a twenty-foot trailer, and a twenty-two-foot whale."

Rae was now in the truck's cab. Randolph was trying to push the wheels back on the road and Jesse was spraying Willy down. Everyone was splattered with mud and water, and scared silly.

"We're running out of water," Jesse shouted.

"It's no use," Rae called from the cab.

Randolph put his hands on his hips and nodded sadly. "We have definitely hit some kind of low here. No question about it."

"We need help," Rae said.

Jesse turned and stared into the tow truck's cab. The red light on the CB was on. . . .

Not knowing what else to do, Glen and Annie waited at the truck stop in the hope that some trucker might have seen a tow truck pulling a whale through the night. While Glen talked to the truckers, Annie sipped a Styrofoam container of coffee at the counter. Suddenly the CB monitor on the wall crackled to life and she heard Jesse say, "Glen? . . . Annie? . . ."

It took less than five minutes for them to find the tow truck and trailer on the forest road. Glen and Annie skidded to a stop and jumped out of the car.

"Jesse! Are you all right?" Annie cried, running toward him.

"What the devil are you doing with my truck?" Glen shouted. "And this whale? This has got to be the craziest thing I've ever seen."

"They tried to kill Willy," Jesse explained while Rae wet the whale down with the pump. "So we're putting him back in the ocean."

Jesse could see that Glen didn't believe him.

"Please," he begged. "You have to help us get him into the water. I'll do anything for you. I swear."

"What do you think I want from you?" Glen asked.

"I don't know," Jesse said. "I don't know what you want." He felt tears start to roll down his cheeks again, but he couldn't help himself. "I have to look out for Willy. I have to do what's best for him. Understand?"

Glen nodded. He could see how much this kid cared for that whale. "Okay, Jesse, there should be a ten-foot chain set behind the front seat. Go get it."

Jesse ran to Glen and hugged him. Glen smiled and looked over to Annie. Pleased, Annie returned his smile. Using the tow truck's winch and Annie's car, they started to drag the trailer back toward the road. Rae used the last of the water in the portable pump to spray Willy down. Jesse stood on the trailer beside the whale, patting his head softly.

"Don't worry," he whispered, "it's going to be okay. Glen's working on it. We're going to get you out of here, Willy."

They managed to get the trailer's wheel out of the mud and slide a board under it. A few moments later, the trailer was back on the road. Rae, Randolph, and Annie jumped into the tow truck's cab with Glen. Jesse got up on the trailer again.

As they headed back up the road, Rae looked through the back window at Willy. "He's getting really dry. We have to wet him down completely.

The sun will be up soon. We don't have much time."

"I know a place," Glen said, making a sudden left.

Back in the trailer, Jesse looked up over the cab to see where they were going. When he saw what was ahead, he smiled and gave Willy a reassuring stroke.

"Don't worry, big guy," he said. "You're going to take a shower right now."

A moment later, Glen pulled the trailer through a truck wash. In the back, Jesse shielded his eyes and he and Willie were sprayed with water. As the truck and trailer came out of the truck wash, a couple of men clutching wine bottles and wearing tattered clothes stopped and stared.

"Hey, nice whale," one of them shouted.

"Thanks," Randolph yelled back.

The sun was starting to come up. In the gray light of dawn, Jesse could see that Willy didn't look well. Jesse bit his lip and tried to be encouraging. "Hang in there," he said. "We're almost home."

Willy's eyes fluttered strangely and he moaned. Jesse had never seen him do that before. "We gotta hurry!" he shouted into the tow truck's cab. "Willy's not doing so good!"

"The marina's just around the corner!" Glen shouted back.

They came around the corner and instantly

slowed down. Jesse spun around and looked over the cab. Standing in front of the marina's locked gate were Dial, Wade, and a couple of men Jesse didn't recognize. Jesse didn't know what Glen was going to do, but he knew Willy wasn't going to survive out of the water much longer.

"Hurry, Glen!" he shouted. "Please hurry!"

"Can you believe this?" Rae groaned in the cab as she stared at the group of angry men waving for the truck to stop.

"What are you going to do?" Randolph asked Glen.

Glen responded by shifting the truck's gears and mashing down on the accelerator. The truck and trailer suddenly lurched forward and started to pick up speed. Dial's men realized what was happening and dove out of the way just as the tow truck crashed through the metal gate.

Glen quickly turned the truck and trailer around and backed them down the public boat ramp and into the water. The truck was almost completely in the water. Rae and Randolph jumped out of the cab. Wading almost shoulder-deep in the cold water, they started to help Jesse undo the harness. But Willy lay motionless.

"Come on, Willy!" Jesse yelled. "We've got to get you into the water. You have to get to work, big guy. It's your turn."

Dial and his crew had gotten back to their feet

and were running toward the boat ramp. Meanwhile Willy hadn't budged from the harness.

"Let's go, Willy!" Jesse shouted. "You've got to move. You've got a family waiting out there for you."

Dial's men were coming closer. Wade was in the lead. He splashed into the water and grabbed Jesse, pulling him away from Willy.

"Go, Willy!" Jesse screamed. "Get out of here!"

The desperation in Jesse's words seemed to wake something in Willy. The whale blinked and shuddered. A second later, he shook free of the harness and started to slide into the water.

"Darn you!" Wade shouted, shaking Jesse.

"Hey!" Glen charged into the water and grabbed Wade, spinning him around. "Let go of my boy!"

Glen smashed Wade in the face, knocking him backward. Randolph, Rae, and Annie tried to stop the other men.

Free from Wade, Jesse dove toward Willy and slid his hands around the whale's head. "Go, just go!" he whispered.

Willy disappeared into the water.

Suddenly Jesse heard the roar of a boat's engine and bells clanging. Looking out into the marina, he saw a long, rocky breakwater built to protect boats from the ocean waves. The only way out of the breakwater was an opening fifty yards wide.

As Jesse watched in horror, two white fishing boats crossed the opening, laying down heavy nets.

Dial's men had commandeered the boats. Standing on the boat ramp, Dial smiled. There was no way that whale could escape the marina. The opening in the breakwater was only twenty feet deep. The nets from the boats would reach the bottom and snare Willy if he tried to swim through them.

As if he were already aware of this, Willy swam in a wide desperate circle, looking for some other way out.

But there was no other way.

Standing waist-deep in the water, Jesse couldn't believe what he was seeing. They'd come so far. Dial couldn't stop them now. Rae sadly slid her arm around the boy's shoulder to comfort him. But Jesse wasn't finished yet. He wouldn't stop fighting unless they held him down or tied him up. He ran back out of the water and started for the breakwater. Some of Dial's men tried to catch him, but he dodged them as skillfully as he'd once dodged pedestrians on the city streets.

Willy stopped circling and followed Jesse as the boy scrambled over the rocks of the breakwater.

"Willy!" Jesse shouted. "Come on, let's go! You've got to do something! Now!!!"

He stopped at the right spot, extended his arm

straight, then made a fist and slowly spread his fingers.

"I love you, Willy!" Jesse cried.

Willy seemed to smile and whistled back to him.

"Now do it!" Jesse shouted urgently.

A second later, Willy disappeared under the water.

Back near the boat ramp, Glen turned to Rae. "What's he doing?"

"He gave Willy the breach sign," Rae said.

"What's that?"

"It means Willy should jump," Rae said. She knew what Jesse had in mind, but it seemed impossible. She turned to Randolph. "Have you ever seen Willy jump that high or that far?"

Randolph shook his head once. "But you never know. Things can happen."

On the shore, Dial and his men stood still, perplexed by Willy's sudden disappearance. Standing in the water, Randolph closed his eyes and chanted softly to himself. *"Salanaa Eiyung Ayesis."*

Jesse ran back and forth along the breakwater, searching for Willy. Finally he stopped and called. "Come on, Willy, you only have to do it once. Just once!"

Suddenly Willy's dorsal fin broke the surface water on the other side of the marina. Willy was

115

barreling toward Jesse, who held up his fist again and slowly spread his fingers.

"Salanaa Eiyung Ayesis," Jesse prayed as tears of hope and fear streamed down his face. *"Salanaa Eiyung Ayesis."*

Like Natsalane, the Indian brave in the story, Jesse found himself chanting a prayer he'd never heard before. Out in the marina, the rapidly approaching dorsal fin suddenly disappeared again under the surface.

Had Willy chickened out? Rae saw Wade start to smile.

A split second later, the water exploded as Willy rocketed upward right in front of Jesse, sailing like a huge black-and-white bird over the breakwater. As he passed Jesse, the boy reached out and touched the orca's glistening side.

With a huge splash, Willy crashed down into the water on the other side of the breakwater.

He was free! Jesse raised a triumphant fist into the air and tears of joy ran down his cheeks.

"Awesome!" Rae cried from the boat ramp where she and Randolph stood. They gave each other high fives.

Near them, Dial shook his head and muttered, "I hate that whale."

Annie and Glen jogged toward the breakwater. Ahead, they could see Jesse waving toward the spot where Willy had disappeared into the broad blue waters that led to the ocean.

" 'Bye, big guy," Jesse said as he wiped his eyes. "I'll see you sometime, maybe. Anyway . . . you take care!"

Annie stood behind him and listened. Overcome with emotion, she gushed, "Oh, Jesse!"

Jesse turned and smiled. "Hey, thanks, you guys." He and Glen shook hands. "Thanks a lot."

"I knew you could get that whale to jump," Glen said.

Jesse put his arms around them and they hugged each other.

"Let's go home," Annie said.

Epilogue

Several days later, a pod of killer whales burst through the sunbathed waters near a remote forested island in the Pacific Northwest. They leapt playfully, leaving great plumes of spray and splashing with their mighty tails, then called each other with cheerful squeals.

One of them had three distinctive spots under his great white jaw. Willy had found his way home.

About the Author

Todd Strasser has written many award-winning novels for young and teenaged readers. Among his best-known books are *Home Alone* (novelization), *Friends Till the End,* and *The Wave.*

Mr. Strasser is a frequent visitor at junior and senior high schools, where he speaks about being an author, and conducts writing workshops. He lives in a suburb of New York with his wife and children and enjoys going to aquariums.